Within the Fog

CHARLES WELCH

ISBN: 9798699114030

DEDICATION

Mia, thank you

CONTENTS

ACKNOWLEDGMENTS

Thank you to Brennon and Sam for being my earliest readers and providing constructive feedback. Thank you, Anthony, for managing all technology and marketing. Thank you, Jazmine, beautiful work as always. Mia, thank you for putting up with a computer constantly in front of my face. Love you all.

Roanoke Island, Virginia 1587

While she is only 12 years old, she has survived much in her young life. She is one of 115 souls who have sailed across the Atlantic. They have been commissioned to create a settlement in this new world in honor of Queen Elizabeth I. These brave men, women, and children had only been here for months when they realized the severity of this hostile land. The elders had decided that their governor, John White, should return to England to acquire further meats, grain, seed, and other necessary supplies. It will be tough to survive in this hostile land.

They live in a fort called Roanoke which they built for their protection. The savage natives have attacked them and do not want them here. The surrounding forests are filled with wild animals who are always looking for their next meal. As winter is approaching the fort will protect them from predators and the elements. She hopes that Governor White will return soon. Her group of settlers will probably suffer in the winter without the replenishment of these necessities.

The environment in this wild new land created many worries. More troublesome though are the strange things have been happening around Roanoke. She notices that crosses, made of simple twigs and leaves from the surrounding trees, have been appearing on the doors of the homes inside the fort. Her father recently has been on the evening security watch four times a week instead of his normal 2 nights a week. The people in her settlement are worried about something.

She overheard adults, including her parents, whispering of strange happenings around the fort. When the adults noticed children nearby, they stop their whispering and go back to their work and chores. Because of this, last night she had pretended to fall asleep next to the fire as her parents were cleaning up after dinner. She had heard at least a bit of their conversation as her parents settled at the dining table after the dishes were clean. She couldn't hear everything they were saying, but she heard enough to know that their neighbor, William Strong, had a strange occurrence two nights ago. A heavy fog had settled over the settlement that night. The fog alone was a harbinger of bad things to come, but much worse was what happened during that foggy night. Apparently, someone had been knocking on William's door, asking to be let into his home. William had refused.

Upon hearing this, she had been confused. Why wouldn't William let any of the Roanoke settlers into his home? She had peered through barely open eyes at her parents who had been huddled around the table. It was difficult to hear their whispers. She could determine William refused the man entry because the man wasn't one of them. Whoever had been at his door was an Englishman who William didn't know. William didn't recognize the voice on the other side of his door. He was a stranger. Her parents were worried because it wasn't possible for an unknown Englishman to be knocking on anyone's door here. The settlers in the colony knew each other, and there were no other settlements. Their fort on the island of Roanoke was the only one of its kind in the new world. The man had refused to identify himself and had kept asking to be let inside William's home.

From what she could interpret of her parent's whispers, her mother was convinced that one of the women in the settlement was a witch. Willa was further worried that they had no garlic with which to place over the threshold of their small home. That explained all the fashioned crosses

3

appearing on doors. It is common knowledge of the God-fearing men and women in the settlement that garlic kept all forms of evil away. If there was no garlic, a cross above a door was an adequate replacement. On the list of goods that Governor White was to return with, was garlic. A request made specifically by her mother.

On this calm October day, she has been playing outside with several of her friends. They have been playing ring around the rosy and several of their favorite games. The day wears down until the afternoon sun begins its slow descent, giving way to the dominion of the moon and the night sky. She and all her friends know better than to argue with their parents when they are told it is time to come in for the night. Torches burn at the tops of the walls of the fort each night as a warning to the hostile natives. They know that the settlers are on guard and armed with munitions, which the natives do not have. Her father has warned her many times to stay within the walls of the fort during the daylight hours. At night she is to stay inside of their home. There is much to fear in the wilderness beyond their walls. Wolves, wild boars, and mountain lions are all aspects of this environment one did not have to fear living in London. She often wonders about the sanity of her parents for wanting to come to this land. It is an honor bestowed upon them to have been selected by the queen, but it is a harsh existence living in this settlement of honor.

"Becca, come in for sup now." She hears her mother call to her. She and her friends are inspecting the carcass of a dead raven. The mysteries of the dead bird are quickly forgotten, and Becca and her friends retreat to their humble homes before the darkening sky.

With night fully settled over them, Becca shivers inside a thick wool blanket next to her mother. Her mother had been teasing her about one boy in the settlement. Becca has a fondness for this lad, but she would never admit it to either of her parents. That subject was still one of embarrassment at her age. A fire burns across from her and her mother, but it does not entirely keep away the chill of the evening Virginia air. Commonly, they keep the fire burning throughout the night hoping to vanquish the ever-present chill. Since the summer had given way to the fall, the cold had invaded their small, two-room structure. A wind that was not present earlier now blows and drafts through their home, and she hopes none of her family will catch a cold. A cold can be a death warrant in this place.

She is getting ready to tell her parents that she will retire to her small straw bed in the backroom when the three of them perk up at the sounds of gunshots.

"Father?"

Her father looks concerned and jumps across the room to retrieve his rifle from the shelf it sits upon.

"Let us not panic just yet, probably ol' Shines shooting at a wolf who has come a little too close to the wall. I'll go see." Ol' Shines was the settlement nickname given to Mr. Shine, who was the oldest member of the settlement party at the age of forty and five years.

As her father approaches the door to remove the wooden bar that obstructs entry into their home there is a knock at the door. Her father hesitates, as one cannot be too careful with the lives of loved ones in this world.

"Hello, speak." Her father cocks his head and tries to listen above the wind gusts for a response. He waits and still, they cannot hear a response after what feels like a full minute.

"I cannot hear ye above this wind. Can ye answer me again? Who calls?" She and her mother sit still so that her father can hear their caller. Again, there is no response. Through the wind they all hear another shot from a rifle, and then another. Then there is yelling, followed by screaming. "Willa, the two of ye get under the blankets in the corner with the butcher knife. We're under attack by the savages."

"But what of the caller?" Willa, her mother, looks to have aged several years in the last few moments.

"Twas probably a warning to us. I need to help with the fight. Be safe within these walls until I return." With that, her father removes the wood plank barrier and opens the door. For a moment the wind howls through the small room and then suddenly it is as still as was that afternoon in the fort courtyard.

As she looks past her father into the dark, a shroud of thick fog drifts into their room. The fog carries with it a smell that has become all too familiar here in this new world. It is death. All sound and winds stop and her father, puzzled, turns to say something to them but his words never come forth. From the darkness beyond him, from within the fog, a pale arm stabs out of the darkness and into his chest, impaling him. It is as if a javelin has been hurdled through the dark, but this implement of death is an arm, attached to a pale, tall, bald man.

The man steps into their home, driving her father back with ease as her father gulps and gurgles his surprise. He looks to the arm buried in his chest and blood spills from his mouth, down his chin. The rifle falls to the floor. Her mother screams as her father looks into the eyes of the man in front of him. The man's eyes are black. They are coals within the sockets of his skull, and he is a vision worse than any nightmare she has ever had when sickened with fever.

The man wears black clothing as dark as his eyes and his mouth opens impossibly wide. His mouth seems made entirely of teeth as long and sharp as knives. Before she can scream a warning, the pale man launches himself into her father like a striking snake. In one bite, he tears most of her father's throat away. The blood stops flowing from his mouth and begins flowing instead in an endless stream from the shredded skin and tissue at his throat. She recognizes that her father has entirely left this world as his body hangs limp on the arm of the man that protrudes from his chest. Her mother is screaming something over and over and finally, her shock abates enough to recognize her name in those screams.

"BECCA!! BECCA RUN!"

She immediately knows her mother wants her to go through the small wooden trapdoor in the floor under the rug in the back room. She springs to her feet and thinks she will grieve the loss of both of her parents later. Her mother is also going to die at the hands of this devil. She must not die. She must be here when Governor White returns to tell him of this murdering fiend.

As she runs to the bedroom, she hears the deepest, most wicked laugh of her brief life, and a voice that is rougher than the harshest of dry summer ground.

YES! Run Becca, run as far as your little legs can carry you. But fear not child. Those legs will never grow long enough to outrun me or my brethren. For we are the darkest corner of the darkest night and I am he who feeds upon the supple flesh of man. Run child, hide under the feces of the swine you feed upon, but I will smell your human reek. I will find you and make you the last meal of this night. I am Croatoan. I am the God of this and every night. And soon Becca, I will be your God.

Becca slides across the floor, throws aside the rug, and tosses open the hatch to the underbelly of their wooden home. She falls through imagining the talons of the pale man narrowly missing her hair as he slashes at the empty air. Without looking back to see if the devil is on her tail, she scoots under the house and peeks out into the fort courtyard. There are people all about, and there is much more than one devil. The monsters are everywhere, and they are devouring her friends and the friends of her parents. People are crying out for their family members, but none can find each other. The fog is too thick. The sounds of another gunshot cracks the air and from under her house, she can see the shot hit one devil in the chest. It laughs at whoever fired the shot and leaps through the air at Anne Minter. With one swing of its arm, Anne's head is separated from her body and the devil wraps its mouth over her open neck. It takes Becca takes a moment to realize that it is drinking Anne's blood.

Becca knows now that none of them will survive this fight. These demons are impossible to kill. They have come here straight from the pits of hell. They are killing, drinking blood, and eating the bodies of everyone in the settlement. The screams go on and on, but the devils continue to murder and consume. She knows there is only one thing she can do. Relinquishing any thought of survival or protection, Becca sprints past Eleanor Dare, who is sobbing at the feet of a devil. The devil is devouring her infant daughter, Virginia. The baby is dead and Eleanor will soon be as dead physically as she is spiritually. Virginia had been the first baby born in this world and now will be the last as people are dying and being eaten all around her.

Becca rounds the corner of the furthest home from the entry of the fort and slams into the large oak tree that grows inside the walls of Roanoke. Pulling the knife her father had given her, she carves one word into the tree as fast as she can. She works furiously as the sounds of gunshots and screaming are fading. As she finishes the last letter in the word she carves, all sound seems to fade. She knows who it is that has come upon her from behind. She can feel the cold drifting off his pale skin. Her temple itches as though a bug has burrowed into her brain and she cannot keep herself from scratching at her head.

Becca, my delicious little piglet, I am flattered and honored.

The devil glances past her to her work on the tree.

Thank you for honoring me. I will make you an offer very few receive. Agree to join me, and you will live amongst us forever with powers you will not believe. Say my name and I will make you immortal. You will never fear death.

Becca turns to face him, staring him in the eyes, refusing to look at the teeth extending from his mouth. "I do not have to fear death even now, devil, for I will live with my slain family in the heavenly ever after. One day on earth living as you, with you, would feel like an eternity of the worst death. And so, I will choose a death that will be by my hand, not yours." And with that, Becca draws the knife across her throat and falls at his feet.

He looks at the life pouring out of her into the ground.

Such a shame. You would have been a rare treat.

He runs his hand across the letters of his name carved into the oak tree and suppresses the anger he feels burning through him. She was to be a part of their future or his final feeding on this night. She has taken both options from him, leaving only a warning to future settlers of his power and existence.

She wasn't angry enough to live amongst us.

Not the ending he wanted to this night, but he would accept it and live to feed again. He would leave her carcass to the others of his kind to consume. Not a drop of her physical existence would remain, unlike him, the one true master of the darkness.

How long will my name haunt these woods, he wonders? He looks one last time at the carving in the oak tree and then walks away, leaving Becca's crumpled form, wasted, at the base of the tree.

Croatoan.

IT BEGINS

The boy knows before he even gets up from his bed that the man is back at his bedroom window. A quick look at his digital alarm clock tells him it is the same time as the past two nights he has woken up feeling this way. He feels stressed and confused and guilty. The man had been at his window the previous two nights and each time the man came he spoke to Bobby. He can only remember that the man wanted Bobby to let him inside the house, although he heard him with his mind, not his ears. The message tonight was the same as it had been.

Let me in.

He gets out of his bed and looks at his window. The blinds are drawn shut, and sure enough, he can see the outline of the man. He had only seen the man unobstructed the first night he had appeared. After that night Bobby keeps the blinds shut, even in the daytime. He tries to shake the feeling that he has done something wrong. The guilt continues to work its way through his mind.

The usual old house noises he has grown accustomed to since moving here have gone quiet, as they have each time the man has appeared. The house is quiet. He can't hear the wind rustling the trees outside or the sounds the old house makes when it objects to the force of that same wind. When the man comes to his window, he can't hear anything other than his ancient voice which sounds deep, and slightly scratchy.

Let me in and I will help you feel better. You've been a terrible young man and have much to atone for.

The voice was getting louder in his head, as it had each night. The boy stares at the silhouette outlined against his blinds and remembers the face he had seen that first night. The man had enormous eyes that appeared black. It was a black so empty that he thought to himself, dead; they are dead eyes. His eyes contrasted with his skin, white like freshly fallen snow. So pale that he could swear that he had seen veins under the man's skin as though it were translucent.

The man had not once tried to get in, instead demanding the boy let him inside. He remembered the first night that he had run terrified from his room. He had glanced back at his window as he turned into the hallway and the man had still been there but had not moved his eyes or head to follow him. He had just continued to stare expressionless into the middle of the room.

Let me in little pig. You've treated your parents horribly. They told you specifically not to play with Timmy Spokes and yet, there you were at the end of the school year playing with him at recess. And why? Because you knew your parents couldn't see you. He's a bad kid, and this is something you also knew to be true, even though you lied to your parents about Timmy.

He is frozen in place. Somehow this makes sense. He did lie to his parents. Timmy was constantly in trouble, but he was fun. Sometimes Timmy did things that went too far. Like when he had lifted Rhonda Sykes dress in the lunch line, and everyone had seen her underwear. Timmy had pretended that James Henderson had been the one to lift her dress. Despite James' pleas of innocence, the school principal wouldn't listen to him, his innocence was denied, and James had gotten in big trouble. But Bobby knew Timmy was the one who had done it and had said nothing. He felt terrible about it, but he had never told the truth, even when the school principal had asked him what he saw. He had looked Mr. Billings right in the eyes and claimed to have seen nothing. Timmy did things like that all the time, and even though it was wrong, a part of him found the exploits of Timmy exciting. It had pissed him off to be told who his friends could and couldn't be, so he had kept right on hanging out with Timmy at school.

And now he felt terrible. The scary man at his window was right, he was a terrible kid. If he let the man in, maybe he would help him talk to his parents. That made sense, and he should go downstairs and open the door so the man could come in, although…. Wait, he thinks, the man is scary. Why would he let in a scary man? He shouldn't do that without asking his parents first. They had told him a million times to never let in a stranger.

Bobby, open the door. It will help. I will explain to your parents that Timmy isn't as bad as they thought. I'll tell them you have been staying away from him. I'm very good at explaining these things to parents.

Bobby pauses. He considers that maybe the man can get his parents to believe Timmy is a good kid. If they believe the man about Timmy, they can play, and he'll be there when Timmy does fun things…. except those things are wrong, and it's why he feels guilt. He should not have ignored his parent's demands regarding Timmy. He had wanted to be friends with Timmy because Timmy was fun, but even more so because his parents had forbidden it. Sometimes he gets mad and stubborn and it makes him do stupid things. He also knows that he is not ever supposed to let in strangers, and the scary man is a stranger. He shouldn't be at my window in the middle of the night either. It's creepy. And those black eyes. They're wrong. And the man is…wrong, very wrong.

"No, I'm not letting you in, go away," Bobby says this out loud in his room with conviction. He needs to be a better kid before the next school year.

Don't be a little shit, Bobby. Let me in the Gods be damned house and do it NOW!

"No." Bobby knows the scary man is getting angry. The feelings of guilt he had awoken with are diminishing and fear is taking their place.

You fucking let me in the FUCKING HOUSE, and you do it NOW or I swear I will see you hanged with your little throat slit. And Bobby, I'll be the one under you drinking every drop of your blood!

18

This is different, and it gets his legs moving. He had heard nothing before tonight other than why he was a terrible kid and demands to be let inside. He runs to his closed bedroom door, which had been open when he fell asleep earlier in the evening and throws it open. As he rounds the corner into the hallway, heading for his parents' room.He can tell the man's voice is fading but the message will not fade, not for his entire life.

LET ME IN! After I eat you, I will pick the splinters of your bones from my teeth.

The voice in his head laughs as it fades, and he screams for his mother as he runs.

ARRIVAL

1

"Hi there Mr. Prepper, I'm going to run into town. We need water and I need my happy pills. Do you need anything?"

Tom Benton looks up at his wife. "You should grab more water than you normally buy and grab some canned meats. Maybe some chicken, tuna, that sort of thing. We have plenty of canned veggies, but we are short on meats. I thought I had more than I do down here. I should start keeping an inventory."

Sandy Benton knows there is no point in arguing with her husband of twelve years. When he concentrates and gets wrinkles across his forehead, he is far too lost to whatever plans and ideas he has to argue with him. She can see those wrinkles developing as he speaks. He is very serious about making sure they are stocked up for the end of the world. Despite her best efforts to keep the stockpiles of food and supplies from over-taking their home, they continue to accumulate. He does not understand that sometimes their dinner has come entirely from his basement 'end of the world' supplies. She loves him for planning for their safety, but she tries to limit how much clutter accumulates in the basement. Occasionally she uses some of his food supplies before they can expire and need to be thrown out. She muses to herself that all married couples must accept certain traits in their spouses. This is better than becoming frustrated. Frustration can lead to bitterness and potentially. a divorce. This prepping for the end of the world is what she has accepted about Tom. He will always plan for the possibility that some trigger-happy dictator will push the big red nuke button and end the American dream. And if that day comes, she and her son will live out their remaining years here in the basement with spiders as the family's only company.

"Sands, I think eventually we need to invest in a generator. I know it's an additional expense and you think it isn't necessary, but imagine even a catastrophic weather event. If we lost power for over 2 or 3 days, I think we would be in some trouble." As Tom says this the wrinkles deepen across his forehead and he paces back and forth in front of the basement shelves that hold his supplies. She loves watching him in these moments because it

21

has always reflected his love and commitment to her and their son. She can see in him the man that would do anything necessary to keep them safe, and it is the reason she fell in love with him.

She reaches out and grabs his shoulder to turn him to her, "As soon as we can afford to, we can get the generator. I know it would be very nice to have if something ever happened. It might be a couple of months yet, but we will figure it out. Around here, as long as we dodge the occasional tornado, we should be just fine. Why don't you quit worrying over the end of the world for a bit and worry a little more about the lawn mowing? Maybe you can do that while I'm in town? The biggest threat I see right now is the lawn growing so tall that we are stuck in the house for the rest of our lives."

Tom laughs a little despite his concerns. His wife has been on him for several days to mow the grass in front of the house. Her concerns about their lawn have always amused him. She is intent on keeping the grass in front of the house cut. Meanwhile, the acres surrounding their house are filled with bushes and brush that can get as high as four or five feet. Their nearest neighbors are a mile north of them, so they don't even have to worry over what the neighbors think.

As if reading Tom's mind Sandy says, "And before you say it again, the grass is different than the weeds and brush around us. People are expected to keep their lawns cut."

Tom doesn't mention this failed previous argument with his wife because she didn't want country living when they purchased this home. He was the driving force behind their move here. Tom felt it was better for the health of his marriage to accommodate her on the lawn mowing issue. Initially, this had been quite a transition for them after living in Denver for so many years. Now an hour east of Denver, in the plains of Colorado about 5 minutes north of the small town of Wray, Colorado, he is living in his version of paradise. A small town with one grocery store, a gas station, two small café type restaurants, and the typical farm stores and mom and pop shops you would expect. And even though Sands (his nickname for her since their second date) preferred the hustle and bustle of the city, she had accommodated his desire to leave it all behind. He was grateful enough for her sacrifice that he would damn well keep the lawn trimmed as she wished. He made good money working from home as a remote learning and development manager for a national company. His income was more than enough for this lifestyle in the country. and the best part was that he worked from home so he could get as much time with his wife and son as possible. As a result, he had become good at expressing his gratitude to his wife by doing the chores around the house she deemed to be important.

Tom reaches around his wife and pulls her into one of his famous bear hugs, "Yes ma'am, I'll mow the lawn as soon as I finish up down here." Sandy gazes up into her husband's blue eyes and remembers the first time she saw them. They are the color of the daytime sky over the Atlantic Ocean of her youth. "Nope, you'll mow the lawn after you speak with Bobby."

Tom looks at Sandy and knows exactly why she wants him to talk to their son. He sighs, "Yeah, I'll talk to him. This seems to have come out of nowhere."

"Maybe it's just a stage, but this is three nights in a row that he has slept in between us instead of his room. All he will tell me is that he sees a scary man outside of his window." Sandy pauses for a moment, remembering her conversation with Bobby, "He knows that his bedroom is on the second floor so no one could really be there, but he is quite convinced."

24

Tom laughs, "So he knows people can't float twelve feet above the ground, and yet he still thinks someone is looking in his room in the night?"

"Yes, Mr. Prepper man, so hurry down here. It's Saturday, and I thought we could have some fun ourselves tonight." She looks at the question written on Tom's face and winks, "Adult fun if you get my meaning. So, our son will need to stay in his bed tonight!" Sandy smacks her husband on the rear end and turns on her heel to go up the basement stairs as he grabs her hand and stops her.

"Well, Mrs. Benton, we seem to find ourselves alone down here, so....."

"Yes, and if I linger any longer down here Sanders Market will close. Then we won't have any water, canned meat, or my happy pills to survive the end of the world."

Tom smacks his wife's butt and tells her, "Off then young lady, we will not die of thirst down here at the end of the world, but lookout tonight. I'll be remembering this conversation!"

Sandy laughs and pats her husband on his cheek, "So will I, as long as you convince our son to stay in his damn bed."

Within the Fog

26

2

Tom sits on a stool in front of what he considers the most important investment he has made in recent years. Not an investment that he expects a monetary return on, it's the type that he hopes he gets no kind of return on at all. All you need to do is spend 15 minutes watching any of the national cable news networks. You can see the potential for so many things to go wrong in the world. So many things to go wrong that would make the money he has put into the supplies in front of him his most important investment. Just last night he was hearing a report of some new coronavirus in Wuhan China that could soon spread around the world. Tom speculates that this is unlikely, as the world has seen many of these types of threats come and go. Despite this, he feels, in his lifetime, everything sitting in front of him will become necessary. The world has grown too large, technology has grown too fast, and the difference between those who have and those who have nothing has become too great. History has shown many times over that these circumstances lead to a rising of the underprivileged minority and war. So, he has little by little accumulated what he can. Sandy thinks he is at least a little crazy, and Tom understands why, but she loves him and that's good enough for him. He prays every day that what he has stockpiled is enough if they need these things, and he also prays that they never need them at all. He made his wife promise him when he began accumulating these supplies that she would tell none of their friends or neighbors. In emergencies, even the closest of friends could quickly become the most severe of enemies. In an emergency, he didn't want knowledge of his stockpile to make him and his family targets for an invasion of their home. He has canned foods, MRE's that his cousin sent him, water (low), blankets, batteries, a propane stove, a crank handheld ham radio (scarce), backpacks, flashlights, medical kit, gun (Glock 19 handgun), 9mm ammunition, knives, and a taser. Sands didn't love the weapons in the house, but he kept them locked in a fire-safe down here in the basement and he had convinced her of their necessity.

Sandy stressing out about the weapons wasn't the only thing she stressed about. She joked often about her happy pills, but those pills, Xanax, had probably saved their marriage. Something had happened to Sandy after Bobby was born. He had watched her deteriorate before his eyes, withdrawing further and further into a dark cloud that only she could see. She was inconsolable and stressed over things that had never bothered her before. Although Tom loved her more than anyone he had ever known, it had been harder and harder to take. Their relationship had been falling apart as they fought and argued over everything. He had constantly tried to get her to see the reality of their world instead of the negativity that she related to him. It convinced him she had been robbed of some essential hormone after giving birth and had become someone he didn't know. When she started telling him there was no purpose in life he had decided it was time to get her doctor involved. Her doctor had prescribed the wonder drug that saved their relationship and maybe her life. The important aspect of her medication was her taking it every day. One day of missing the pill wasn't the end of the world as long as she didn't miss more days. The memory of her depression was so ingrained in Tom that he had a habit of asking her if she remembered to take the medication. The few times that she had missed her meds, he had known it before asking her. That old dark cloud returned, and the dullness replaced that shining gleam she usually carried in her eyes. At least today she had remembered her prescription on her own, and he hadn't needed to ask her if it was time to get a refill. Yesterday morning he had caught her alone at the dining table with that faraway look. He had become suspicious of her behavior and by noon he had asked her if she had remembered her pill. She had assured him she was feeling fine, and she had been taking it every day.

Tom grabs the Dynamo Hand Crank Ham radio and begins winding it to check that it still functions properly when he realizes he's probably been lost in thought far too long. He decides he will check the radio as he visits with his son so he can get on the lawn mowing before Sands gets back home. He heads upstairs and calls Bobby from his room.

"What?" Bobby calls down to him.

"I said come downstairs to the front porch, please."

"Why?" Bobby yells down. Frustrated, Tom yells back to his son, "Because I said and doing what I say is good for your health." He can hear Bobby laughing at him and he smiles to himself. His son has always had a great sense of humor, which was why it was so strange to see the panicked little man that had been running to their bedroom the past few nights. Even stranger to see the occasional bursts of anger from Bobby. He's never been a temperamental kid, but lately, they've had to correct some temper tantrums. He suspects that it is the lack of sleep and fear that Bobby has been experiencing.

Tom walks through the living room as the evening light streams through the windows. This is his favorite time of day. He loves being outside when the heat fades and evening settles on the end of another sunshiny Colorado day. From his front porch, he can look west and see the silhouette of the Rocky Mountains. He can walk to the end of the drive, past the trees that border their property, turn to the left and see the town of Wray where Sands has gone to the store. And if he looks right to the north, he can see his nearest neighbor's home. He and Sandy have become good friends with the older couple who live up the road. Steve and Sabrina Sellers have helped he and Sandy out in a couple of situations when they needed sitting for Bobby. He muses to himself; Steve and Sabrina had become the grandparents that Bobby otherwise did not have.

Sitting on the swinging bench on the front porch he is ready at Bobby again when the front door opens and Bobby hops out. "What do you want Dad?"

"I want to visit with you about something." As soon as he says this, he regrets his choice in words. Bobby looks worried. "Relax big man, you're not in trouble. I just wanted to check on something with you."

Bobby swallows hard and a slight breeze ruffles his blonde hair. "What do you want to check on?"

3

Sandy heads south on State Highway 385 toward the town, their town of Wray. The peaceful views in this area of Colorado always fill her with a sense of contentment she had never felt before living here. So much open space, the green fields of summer that fade to gold in the fall. The ancient and wise oak and cottonwood trees that stand solid to offer the protection of their massive limbs. The Rocky Mountains standing like a sentry posted to watch over all who live to the east on the plains. The friendly people who wave a cheery hello. She had not wanted to move here, but she could not have been more wrong about this place. Although she didn't want to admit that to Tom. Why was that? Maybe some little remnant of pride or she wanted him to keep being so accommodating with the domestic responsibilities. Eventually, she would tell him she never wanted to live anywhere else, but not yet.

As for now, it was time to pick up her prescription and a few items before Sanders market closed and get back home. Another thing she didn't want to admit was that she had not taken her Xanax for three days and it was showing. The edges of that dark cloud have been showing. She has had a couple of moments that she could feel its grip, and then it had faded away. For a day she had thought it was okay that she had forgotten the medication. She contemplated that she had outgrown the need for it and didn't need it any longer. And then yesterday morning had rolled around, and she slipped back into that gloom-filled mood that had almost ruined her life. At that point, she realized she had not picked up her refill yet, and Tom had given her that knowing look. She was sure he had noticed yesterday and then, sure enough, he had quizzed her about it. She had lied to him and said she had been taking it because if she didn't, he would watch her like a hawk for days to come. She wanted to enjoy a wonderful weekend with him and Bobby, so the last thing she needed was him worrying over her forgetting to take the medication.

She smiles to herself thinking about the little secrets married couples keep from each other. Sometimes it was good to preserve the marriage. Her thoughts drift back to the present moment and the evening ahead of them. Tonight would be a movie night. Something good was always available. If she hurried, she would have plenty of time to get back to the house before the sun went down in its daily blaze of glory. And getting home before the sun went down was always preferable to driving down 385 in the dark.

As she reaches the first stop sign in town and puts on her blinker to turn west, she notices old Ruth Hilthers shuffling up the sidewalk toward her house off Main street. She wears a blue dress, white knee-high stockings, and shoes that Sandy always thinks of as nursing shoes. As much as Sandy loves this place, she dislikes the judge-mental, snooty Ruth. Sandy didn't have enough fingers and toes to count the number of times that woman had insulted her or Tom. Ruth complained about Bobby being too loud in town at one event or another, even though he was no louder than any other kid. Sandy remembered the time she and Tom had taken Bobby to their first experience with the Wray harvest festival. That day Ruth had walked up and suggested that Sandy invest some time and effort in teaching Bobby proper manners. She had accused Bobby of making the other children unruly.

This coming from a woman who had never had children. Tom had grabbed Sandy's hand and led her away from Ruth that day before she could say something in return, which was wise. She knew from many of Wray's other residents that she and Tom weren't the only targets of Ruth's ire, but it had made her dread the woman. After that day, she had avoided Ruth at all costs. Thankfully, it appeared the old woman was going home, which meant she had just missed running into her in the market. Sandy parks her Outback in front of Sanders Market, and strides into the store, waving hello to Mr. Sanders, the owner, on her way inside.

"Evenin' Sandra."

It had been Sandra from the beginning, no matter how many times she tried correcting Mr. Sanders. Sandy wasn't short for anything else. It was Sandy on her birth certificate, but after a while, she had given up. With Mr. Sanders, she is Sandra.

"Hello Mr. Sanders, I won't be too long. I only need a couple of things."

Mr. Sanders smiles at her and waves a hand dismissing her concern, "Take your time, dear, get what you need."

Sandy makes her way from isle to isle, remembering Tom's concern about the state of their bottled water supply. She loads three, thirty-six packs of water in her cart, and several cans of canned chicken and tuna. She even grabs another small propane canister, thinking how pleased Tom will be that she is taking his efforts seriously. Finally, she stops in front of the pharmacy counter in the back of the store. After a short and pleasant chat with the pharmacist, Ellie Pearson, she has her prescription and can make her way to the front of the store to check out with Mr. Sanders.

As he scans the grocery items, she finds her attention drifting to the parking lot beyond the large store-front windows. In the back of her mind, she can hear Mr. Sanders chatting with her about something that seems important, but she can't escape what she is seeing in the parking lot. She can't figure out what bothers her about the view through the store windows, as nothing is wrong or out of place, but something is….off. That's it, something is off, or different seeming. In the pit of her stomach, Sandy feels it more than she is aware of it and it bothers her. She feels like she had something to eat that didn't quite agree with her stomach, even though she has had nothing to eat since this morning. If this was another consequence of not taking the Xanax, she needs to take it as soon as she gets home.

"… and so I told him well you better drive on up to the Benton's and ask them yourself so he may stop by to see you. Sandra, are you alright?"

Sandy realizes that she's being rude. She is still staring through the store windows in front of her Subaru and can't put her finger on what seems wrong. The pit of her stomach tells her that the feeling isn't related to food at all, but dread. Possibly the lack of her medication, but it doesn't feel like that. She rationalizes this feeling and tells herself to quit being weird. No scary movies for them tonight.

"I'm sorry, Mr. Sanders, I don't mean to be rude. I can't quite figure out what seems off outside. Look out there, does something seem different to you?"

Mr. Sanders looks up over the rims of his wire-framed glasses and follows her gaze out the store windows. He immediately responds to her, "It's getting dark far too early. I wonder why that would be. Shouldn't be getting dark like this for another hour, but sure enough, the sun is already fading. Maybe a storm is rollin' in, sure hope we don't get hailed."

A little voice inside Sandy tells her that Mr. Sanders is right, and he is wrong. She knows this as soon as he tells her it's getting dark too early. He is right, that's exactly what is bothering her. The light differs completely from when she had driven in and parked here moments before. It's darker, and it shouldn't be, yet he is wrong about a storm. She has never seen the sunlight look like this here. The light outside almost has that fall type of tint to it, but much darker and this is the middle of July. A pending storm is not the cause of this, hail, or no hail.

"Yeah, you're probably right, just a storm rolling in and right back out," Sandy is not willing to let the fear gnawing at her gut show. Is this a simple anxiety attack coming on from not taking her medication? Again, she tells herself no, this feels nothing like being off of the Xanax.

"Well, that's the strangest thing isn't it? Might be a big storm to look like that out there."

Sandy couldn't care less about the water and other items now resting in the cart as she hands Mr. Sanders two twenty-dollar bills. If she didn't need her medicine, she would get the hell out of here and get home now. It is as if the devil himself has tapped her on the shoulder.

Mr. Sanders continues to peers over his glasses as he slowly grabs her change from the cash register drawer. He's reaching to hand her the change when he drops a quarter on the floor. "Darn it, fingers ain't what they used to be, like the rest of me I guess." He bends down to find the quarter and Sandy shuffles her feet. The voice of anxiety whispers in her ear. Dammit, he needs to hurry up, she thinks as he knocks over a dirty fly swatter. It falls to the floor in front of the quarter that he cannot see.

"It's okay Mr. Sanders, Tom wanted me back quick today, we have so much going on at home I don't need the quarter."

He looks up at her and shrugs her comments off, "Nonsense, I haven't ever shortchanged a customer in thirty years, and I won't start now, let me just grab you a different quarter from the drawer." Sandy feels the need to run from the store building in her. Her breath comes shallow and rapidly. This is irrational, she thinks to herself. This is not the anxiety issue she has had in the past. No, this is different, almost intuitive. She needs to get out of the store and she knows it. Finally, as she is considering for the hundredth time running out the door, Mr. Sanders locates another quarter in his drawer and hands her the change.

"Need any help today? That bottled water can get heavy." Mr. Sanders looks at her for an answer, but she is already moving the cart toward the door as she hollers a no thank you over her shoulder. She is so focused on getting out the door that she just registers Mr. Sanders saying, "Well I'll be, would you look at that?"

Sandy stops, and looks back at the store owner and follows the track of his eyes, which appear to be looking at her car. She gazes out and realizes she can't see her car. She can't see anything. The day is gone, and most of the light with it. For a moment she feels like the entire world has melted away into a never-ending void, and then she realizes what she is seeing.

She and Mr. Sanders both utter the same word "fog."

4

"Well Bobby, you have had a couple of rough nights lately and I wanted to see what's going on." Tom wants to be relaxed about this so that Bobby will be too. Bobby looks out at trees that lightly sway. The breeze bending the trees seems to come from the direction of town. He looks as though he is remembering something that genuinely scared him, and he looks older than his eight years.

As Tom is ready to bring it up again Booby sighs, "something has scared me I guess, and it makes me not want to be in my room at night." He looks relieved that he has finally expressed his fear out loud., As if a weight has come off his shoulders.

"What's got you scared at night?" So far this is going much easier than Tom imagined it would, and he feels some relief. Hopefully, he can tell Sands that they have solved the problem when she returns.

"You'll think I'm making it up and you won't believe me." Tom is surprised by this response, even though he already knows what middle of the night demons his son's very active imagination has created.

"To be honest with you son, your mom told me you mentioned that someone was outside of your window, and….." Tom is abruptly cut off mid-sentence by his son.

"Not someone dad, a scary man!"

"A man? What kind of scary man are we talking about here? Is he old, young, tall, short?" Bobby looks out across distant farm fields, reliving the moments in the middle of the night with his monster.

"I'm not sure. My comics don't have a man like this one. He's more like a monster." Bobby looks as though he must explain this man in the best way that he can. "He is pale and looks like a man with very pointy ears and he has sharp teeth. His eyes are huge dad, so big, but it's almost like he can't see me."

"Why can't he see you?"

"I think he can't see me because when I move in my room his eyes don't follow me. It's like he's trying to see in but can't."

"Bobby, I'm a little confused here. Why would a scary man be looking in your window but not see you? It seems a little silly that he would bother if he can't see you, don't you think? Not to mention Bob, no one could be outside your window because you're on the second floor. There's nothing for anyone to be standing on outside your window." Tom is hoping his son will think this through and find some clarity.

"I'm not sure, dad. I'm not sure how come he can't see me, and I do not understand how he can be there, but I know why he's there."

Bobby says this last part with such conviction that Tom cannot help but ask, "Why is he there?"

"Because he's hungry."

A slight chill crawls its way up Tom's back at his son's response. He tries to push the chill back down where it came from, but it works its way up to the top of his head. It sizzles there for a moment.

"How do you know he's hungry?" As Tom whispers this question, deep inside, in a primitive place from the day's men lived in caves, he knows his son's answer before he speaks it.

44

"Because he told me, dad. He wants me to let him in because he wants to eat us."

5

"Mr. Sanders? How could it become foggy so fast? That didn't take two minutes to go from getting dark outside to fog. Has this happened here before?"

Mr. Sanders contemplates her question as he stares into the fog. For the first time, he has the look of a man lost for an answer. "I ain't never seen this here or anywhere."

Sandy still can't shake the feeling that she needs to leave, she needs to go home, and she needs to do these things now, but getting her legs to agree is going to take some effort. Mr. Sanders looks at her as if seeing her for the first time this day, "Fog is fog I suppose, but we had ourselves a hot July day, Sandra. Not a cloud in the sky, no rain, nothing. So why do we have fog? It's unnatural. Don't feel right, atall. Jesus, Mary, and Joseph, if this ain't the damnedest thing."

Sandy doesn't know much about how weather events get created, but she instinctively agrees with him on one point. This is not right. She can remember an event from her childhood.

Something she has never shared with anyone, including Tom. She had been about Bobby's age. It was a morning before school, one week after her grandmother had passed away. Her grandmother was the person who had most influenced her in her early years. She still held her in the highest esteem. She had been in her room getting ready to brush her hair when she had welled up with tears at the memory of the many times her grandmother had sat and brushed her hair. She would tell Sandy stories of days gone by. It was a simple moment they had shared over and over and one that belonged only to the two of them, she and her grandma. As the tears wound their way down her cheeks, she withdrew her hand from reaching for her brush. She didn't want to brush her hair any longer. It was something shared between her and her grandma and she would go downstairs and inform her mother that she wanted her long blonde hair cut short immediately. As she had stood in front of her bedroom mirror the strangest thing had happened. The brush she had been reaching for had slid in front of her as though guided by an invisible touch. She could feel another's presence in that moment. The brush had stopped right in front of her as if to say, "brush your hair." And someone or something had pushed it to her. That memory popped in her mind now. She remembered the feeling of knowing that someone she couldn't see was there beside her. Now she

47

could feel something very similar. Something was here. Not right beside her in the same way as that moment many years before. No, something was in the fog.

"Mr. Sanders, do you see anything out there? I mean, besides fog. I know that sounds stupid, but…". She trails off as she looks at him and knows regardless of his reply, he sees nothing in the fog, but he feels it just the same as she does.

"No, Sandra, I see nothing but I spect you should get on home now, you know, in case this gets worse. Let me help you out."

Sandy knows now is the time to shake this feeling off, at least long enough to get moving. "No, I can handle loading the car, but Mr. Sanders, you all need to go home now too. Like right now. Please don't wait any longer. Head home quickly, ok?" Mr. Sanders looks at Sandy and nods his head once.

6

Tom gathers himself for a moment. For God's sake, he thinks, your son has a great imagination. Someday he should write novels or movie scripts, but for today you need to be the adult here, Tom Benton. It's a story or even a dream Bobby had, and there's nothing more to it. He needed the right response to Bobby, and he needed to come up with that response in short order.

"Bobby, I can remember being your age and having similar bad dreams, but that's all this is. They call them night terrors, and they seem very real, but there aren't any hungry monsters that want to eat us. At least you for sure, you'd taste too sour and chewy." Tom laughs in an attempt at using humor to reassure his son but knows he has fallen flat.

"Dad, it's not a dream. I saw him and I heard him."

Tom reaches for the handheld ham radio and begins winding it. "The thing is Bobby, what you're telling me isn't possible." Tom finished cranking the handle to give the handheld radio some power and flips the power switch to the on position.

49

"I told you."

Tom is scanning through the bands on the radio as he asks his son, "Told me what?"

"That you wouldn't believe me."

That comment hurts. He begins to tell Bobby that night terrors seem real when he faintly catches a man's panicked sounding voice on the radio. He goes backward on the channel switch and finds the man's voice again, although with a lot of static. "…and stay inside. Not sure how many there are, but……. And fast." The man is speaking fast and in an increasingly higher pitch. He speaks as though he has limited time and is trying to say as much as he can. Tom can't get the reception to clear, so the man's voice continues to come through in bits and pieces.

"Dad? Who is that?"

"I'm not sure son, but he can't be all that far away. Sounds a little familiar to me, just someone playing a prank." Bobby was already scared, so he sure didn't need to make this worse. And oh lord, would Sands kick his ass if he was the reason Bobby ended up in their bed again tonight. "Yeah, I'm sure it's a joke someone's playing."

Bobby does not at all look convinced and flatly tells Tom, "No, he's scared."

The voice over the radio comes through again, "They can't come in unless you open up. He was outside my door for the longest time, but I could hear....... My neighbor..... it was....... and OH GOD, I fear she's DEAD!" This last word is the only word to come through crystal clear over the radio.

"Ok, haha, that's enough of this. Someone jerking people's legs a little." Tom snaps off the radio and thinks to himself, shit, the kid will never stay in his bed now. "That's all that was Bobby, just some people messing around. Bored, I guess, no reason for us to keep listening."

As he sets the radio aside another sound comes, and he reaches to pick the radio up again. He stops, in midair.

"It's not coming from the radio dad; it's coming from town."

Tom listens and realizes his son is right. The sound he is hearing is the town's emergency siren, and he immediately thinks about tornadoes until he looks up at a sunny and cloudless sky.

More to himself than Bobby, he asks aloud, "What the hell is going on?"

7

Sandy is sure that the hardest thing she has ever had to do is begin forward momentum, pushing the cart out of the safety of Sanders Market. She moves toward the doors that lead to the parking lot where hopefully her Outback is waiting for her. As the automatic door opens, and she steps forward, she can feel the humidity that has suddenly enveloped the day turned to night. More than the damp feeling against her skin though she notes the slight stench in the fog. It smells a little like the time a mouse had died in a trap Tom had put behind their washer at home. He had failed to check the trap for several days and the laundry room had, not an overpowering stench, but a definite scent of decay. The smell in the fog, like the smell in the laundry room, isn't strong, however, unlike the smell in the laundry room, she knows this isn't caused by a mouse. This smell is deeper, much more earthy. Strange, she thinks, the things that run through your mind when you are scared and feel you need to pee.

At first, her strategy is to slowly move through the fog as silently as possible, although she isn't sure why she's trying to remain invisible. She

53

sides with the little voice in her mind that keeps telling her to find the car and get out of town. She pushes forward on the sidewalk against the building, guessing that within a few steps she will see the silver nose of the Subaru. Sure enough, the headlights and slight grill appear, and she withdraws the remote from her pocket and unlocks the car, popping the hatchback. Maneuvering the shopping cart to the back of the car, she unloads her supplies haphazardly, tossing them into the back. The fear coursing through her veins seems to have replaced her blood. Every time she leans back out of the car, she is convinced she can hear whispers within the shroud of the swirling mist that surrounds her. Straight home, pour a glass of water, and take the damn medicine, she thinks. That's exactly what I'm going to do.

Mr. Sanders would think he was seeing a crazy woman the way she throws items into the Outback. However, judging by the way he had stared into the fog, he wouldn't blame her at all. There was no way he could now see her through the fog, even though she was only ten feet from the windows he had been staring through.

Okay, Sandy muses to herself, now I need the cases of water and I am out of here. She is sliding her hands under the first of the three cases of water when she hears something slide past her in the fog. Whatever it is, it is fast enough that her hair sways in the slight breeze created by its momentum. She stops for a moment listening when the more logical part of her kicks in and she throws the cases of water in the car. When you feel something like that, she reasons, you don't stand still waiting to feel it again. You hurry the hell up and get done. She grabs another case and tosses it into the car. At that same moment she hears and feels something slash past her, this time at her back. It is close enough that she is sure something has brushed against her jeans. Fuck this, she says in her mind and abandons the shopping cart and the remaining case of water. As fast as she can, she slams the rear hatch on the mess of supplies she has thrown in the car and rounds the corner of the vehicle. She reaches for the driver's door handle. The door is open, and she is in. She grabs the interior handle to pull it shut. The door moves three inches and stalls. She pulls again, and it moves no closer to shutting.

"Dammit, what the fuck is happening?" Panic is becoming the largest part of her. Sandy looks down and sees that a jacket she had previously poked under the driver's seat has slid forward enough to get jammed in the door frame. "Shit!" Bending down, she pushes the car door open further with her left hand and tugs the jacket free of the doorjamb with her right hand. The jacket pops loose, and she slams the door shut. hitting the door lock button. She feels relief although her rational mind lectures her. She is no closer to home than she had been. There is no time or reason to celebrate getting in the car when she still has so far to go.

"Okay, breathe. Two blocks ahead, turn left and straight home." Talking to herself out of a need for reassurance more than anything, Sandy backs up and begins the two-block trek back to Highway 385. She is amazed by the density of the fog that surrounds her. She knows that she will need to drive slowly enough to keep from having an accident despite wanting to hit the accelerator. Her goal is to get out of Wray as fast as possible. None of this feels right, and it makes zero sense that there should be fog here today at all. Sandy isn't the conspiracy theorist in the family, a title proudly held by her husband, but her mind continues to work through scenario after scenario as to how the fog has appeared in the middle of summer. And anything that her mind wanted to chew on right now was better than contemplating what she felt in the parking lot. Not taking her Xanax is not responsible for what she felt back there in the fog. Something had touched her. She wanted to believe someone was messing with her and now had a free case of bottled water for their efforts. If that's what is going on, Sandy decides she won't be angry. She will happily share a laugh and a drink with the troublemaker. For now, she decides someone is pranking her, and that is all. This idea is much better than any other alternative.

She is half a block away from the intersection when the town's emergency alarm goes on, shrieking and wailing in its up and down rhythm. Louder and softer, higher and lower in pitch. Why would the emergency system be activated for fog? Not her worry, she decides. I need to get out of here. I can wonder about all of this once I'm safe at home.

"Ok, turn left and I'm on the home stretch," Sandy utters this as she approaches the intersection with Highway 385. She has the turn signal on to turn left when she sees a form in the fog ahead of her. It is moving directly in front of her and in her direction. It gradually takes a human shape and is comprised of dark vapor until she recognizes the shuffle of its steps. "Oh, for Christ's sake, how can this day get worse?" The shuffling continues in her direction. The shadow draws closer until Sandy can make out knee-high white stockings.

"Lovely, Good old Ruth wandering around in the damn fog in the middle of the street. I could have run you down." Sandy says this aloud to the empty interior of her car and whispers a prayer that Ruth will not recognize her. "God knows why she's out here to begin with." Ruth is now visible next to Sandy's car. Much to Sandy's dismay, Ruth stops and stares through the car windows. The old woman mouths words that Sandy cannot hear. For a moment Sandy wonders why Ruth has smudged strawberry ice cream sauce across her forehead and right cheek. Her brain finally sorts out this image and she realizes Ruth is bleeding. Without thinking further, Sandy rolls down the window.

"Ruth are you all right? You're bleeding."

Ruth continues to talk in a low whisper, and Sandy leans toward the open window to hear the old woman. She's speaking too soft to hear over the siren.

"Ruth, what are you saying?" Sandy realizes that although Ruth is seeing her, she is also seeing through her. Ruth is not connected to this moment in time or even with reality. As Sandy leans closer to Ruth to speak to her, the town's alarm cuts off. It startles her more than when the alarm first began its shrieking. Now the world has become too quiet, even though the alarm had only been active for a few minutes.

"You're bleeding. Why don't you get into the car?"

Ruth continues to stare at Sandy and past her, "They wouldn't let me in my house." She is confused, not about what she is thinking but how to say it, "They stink like a bunch of little shit kids who needs changing. I told them that, I said to them you stink, get off my property and get out of my way, but he laughed, and then he god damn hit me. He hit me. That fucker hit me right across my head and he was fast. It hurt, but I got right back up because NO MAN will ever hit me again. I swore it. I swore no man would EVER hit me again over thirty years ago, I swore it God damn it I swore it and that FUCKER HIT ME!!!!!"

Sandy knows that Ruth getting louder and louder is not a good thing. She knows deep inside that it is a terrible thing. "Ruth listen, it's going to be okay, but you need to quiet down and get in the car. Just come around and get in with me okay. Come on Ruth." Sandy is imploring her to get in the car. Ruth is in a state of shock and she is not moving. She is also not getting any quieter. Ruth is hurt and angry and getting louder by the second.

"He HIT ME and HE LAUGHED about it and if I was younger and could see better, I would

have HIT HIM RIGHT BACK!!!" Tears roll down
Ruth's cheeks and are mixing with the blood
coming from her head. Sandy thinks of Kool-Aid.
"My eyes are shit and I couldn't see him well
enough in this fog to describe him but I'm damn
well going to tell the sheriff. HE HIT ME!"

"Ruth, if you keep yelling, he's going to
come hit you again! Now shut the fuck up and get
in the car!" This finally gets through to Ruth, and
for the first time Ruth realizes where she is as she
looks around the street. She reaches down and
smooths her skirt with a shaking hand. Sandy sees
Ruth's pride return to her features.

"Yes, I'll take a ride thank you, but I will
NOT tolerate you yelling at me. Watch your
tongue." Ruth snaps off this last sentence and begins
walking toward the rear of the Outback.

Sandy rolls up her window and mutters,
"That is why I cannot stand you." She watches
Ruth shuffle to the back of the car in her side mirror
and wants to get out and kick her in the ass to make
her hurry up. At last, Ruth is gone from view, so
Sandy switches her gaze from the driver's side
mirror to the passenger side mirror. "Hurry up, you
mean old bitch." Sandy considers the exact words
Ruth had been muttering and yelling. Ruth had

been the victim of a man in the past, which explained her behavior. But Sandy still doesn't feel bad for her. I should try to look past all of Ruth's rudeness by thinking of what she's gone through, but I just can't do it, Sandy reflects on Ruth's attitude. "I don't like her at all and yet, I am sitting here waiting for her to get in the car to give her a ride."

A thought occurs to Sandy that she should have been aware of the minute she told Ruth to get in the car. She was giving Ruth a ride to where, exactly? Ruth had said someone wouldn't let her get into her house, so now what? Delay and try to take her home again? No, someone was out there messing with me while I loaded my supplies from Sanders, she thinks. Now Ruth is saying that a man hit her and wouldn't let her get into her home. There was no way she could drive Ruth home, which meant only one thing, "Oh God." She would have to take Ruth home with her. What would Tom think when she arrived with Ruth Hilsers?

Speaking of Ruth, what was taking so long? Sandy leans forward in her seat and peers into the passenger side mirror. Nothing but the side of the Outback and fog. Damn it, did the crazy old woman wander off? Sandy leans back and thinks, no frickin way. No way am I getting out of this car to see what has happened to her. "Shit!" She waits a few seconds longer holding her breath listening. She hears nothing at all. "Okay, alright, one quick peek," Sandy takes a deep breath and thinks that if Ruth passed out from the blow to her head, she can't just drive away and leave her lying in the road. One quick peek behind the car and if Ruth isn't there, then she's on her own. She reaches down and pulls the door handle and remembers the interior dome light. She doesn't want it to come on. She doesn't want to advertise that she is opening her door, so she quickly pushes the button that keeps the dome light off. She eases the door open. The rank smell of deteriorating flesh is back and seems much stronger than moments before. She pulls the neck of her t-shirt over her nose and puts her left foot out of the car when she freezes. The hair on her arms stands on end. She is sure she heard a muffled whimper, but it was coming from somewhere far away. She listens, holding her foot a few inches above the road surface. There is movement. She struggles to sense where the movement is coming from, but it feels like it is from above her. It sounds like wings cutting the air. Wings, that's what it is, she thinks, wings.

She pulls her foot back in the car. As she does this, she sees a very dark-skinned, weathered hand with long fingers reaching through the fog. She pulls the car door shut. The nails on the hand brush against the door frame and the sound is like a screwdriver scraping metal. The door slams shut, and she throws the car into drive. The Subaru's tires squeal and she sees a large mass fall. It lands with a dull thud a few feet from the front driver's side of the car. In the glow of her headlamps, she can see a foot and ankle with white stockings, sprayed with blood, sticking out of the mass on the road.

"Oh God, oh God, oh GOD!"

Ruth. She looks away knowing that she will get sick. As she puts her foot down on the accelerator, she realizes her door remains unlocked. Locking the door and turning the corner with tires squealing, she no longer cares about having an accident. It is an acceptable risk. She must get away from the fog. She can't allow her mind to consider all that has happened in the last few minutes. She can't consider what is roaming in the fog because all she can think about is whether her husband and son are also stuck in the fog.

8

"C'mon Bobby, let's walk down to the road to see what's going on in town." Tom is a little concerned about his wife being in town now that he can hear the emergency siren. If it weren't for the large bank of elms, oaks, and cottonwood trees lying between his property and the town of Wray he could see the town from his porch. As it is, to see the town, he must walk down his gravel driveway to Highway 385.

Bobby jumps off his seat on the porch step and follows his dad, kicking loose rocks as he goes. Tom reaches the highway which never has much traffic on it. He tells Bobby to stay behind him on the driveway, anyway.

Stepping a little further off his property onto the highway's black surface, Tom gazes to the south, "What is that?" When he can't make sense of what he is seeing, he becomes a little more concerned for his wife. He reaches for his cell phone in his front pocket.

"What is it, dad? What do you see?"

"Well, Bobby," Tom replies as he is dialing his wife's cell phone number, "I can't be too sure, but it looks like there's a big fog bank over the town."

"Wow, let me see dad!"

Tom pinches his phone between his shoulder and his ear and reaches back to hold his sons' hand as he guides him onto the road.

Bobby looks toward town, "Oh yeah, fog, sure enough. That looks exactly like the fog that comes to my window with the scary man."

This gets Tom's attention. "You've seen fog outside your window?" As Tom is asking about his sons' revelation, the emergency siren stops its wailing and the evening becomes silent.

"Dad, why did it stop?"

"I'm not sure but listen to me, Bobby. I want you to be honest. I don't want any lying or exaggeration. Do you understand?" Tom can see by the expression on his son's face that he is okay with this request. "Are you sure you've seen fog outside of your window when you've seen the scary man?"

Bobby doesn't hesitate at all, "That's easy dad. Why would I lie? Every time I see him, fog is all around outside my window." Tom doesn't understand the fog he is seeing. He doesn't understand why Bobby would see fog or the scary man, but he can see that his son is being honest, or at least believes he is being honest. Bobby looks at him like it is the most natural thing in the world that they would see fog in the evening of a warm summer day. Tom can only think Bobby has dreamed of all this in a series of night terror episodes, but it seems a little coincidental that there is now a fog bank over Wray. He can't see any of the buildings in the town, and if he didn't live here and know there was a town down the road to the south, he would have no idea of its existence.

Tom realizes the empty beeping in his ear indicates that his call to Sands didn't go through. He moves Bobby back into the driveway and redials his wife's number. The phone seems to hesitate for a moment, attempting to make the connection, and then he gets the same beeping. His call doesn't connect. Strange, he thinks, and then he considers what he will do if Sands doesn't come back home on time. He will have to drive into town to the market, through the fog, to find her.

"This just doesn't seem right, Bobby." As Tom stares at the fog bank in the distance, he thinks the fog is growing closer to them. "Bobby, does that fog look like it's a little closer to us?"

"Yup, sure does dad, and I bet the scary man is in that fog."

9

Sandy turns the corner onto the highway and glances in her rearview mirror. Before she can decide if she is seeing the outline of someone in the fog, the image retreats into swirls of mist that blend and mix. She thinks she may have seen nothing at all. She decides it is in her best interest to keep her eyes forward in the direction she is heading. Her visibility is limited to ten feet or less and she is driving way too fast for conditions. She reasons to herself that she needs to only clear two blocks of the town and then the very short mile to her house. She feels relief as she drives through the last intersection in town. In a matter of only seconds, she will be away from Wray with only fields, trees, and brush on either side of the road. Much more appealing than vehicles, sidewalks, and buildings while navigating the fog. Sandy recognizes Saint Mary's catholic church when the fog parts for a moment. She can see the stately old building with its stone façade through the mists if the fog. The church is the last building at the edge of town and Sandy mentally prepares to slow down now that she is leaving town. As she passes the church, she feels as though she has transitioned from one world to another. The fog is completely gone and the sunny

July evening that she had driven through to go to the market returns. For a moment the sun blinds her, and she holds a hand to the side of her head to block the sunlight. She lets out a sigh of relief and instead of slowing down; she presses even harder on the gas pedal.

Within the Fog

10

"Bobby, let's go back up to the house so I can try to get a signal on my phone." Tom walks back up the driveway but hesitates when he hears a vehicle. He turns back to the highway. Bobby turns with him. Glancing back toward the town, he notices two things. First, sunlight glances off a vehicle, and he becomes certain that it is his wife. She appears to be driving fast. He can see the silver color of the vehicle and it looks about the size of Sands Outback. He also becomes convinced that, yes, the fog has grown closer. "Bobby, that's your mom coming, let's get up to the porch and wait for her."

Bobby mumbles his agreement and sprints ahead of his dad to the house. Tom watches his son leap over a weed growing along the edge of the lawn and remembers he was supposed to have been mowing. Well, I'll help unload the car and then I'll mow. As long as it gets done, he reasons.

11

As Sandy approaches the driveway to her house, she can tell that the evening is fading and will soon give way to the night. A natural night, she thinks, the kind of night that has followed day since the beginning of time. Not the false darkness she experienced in town. As she turns into the long gravel driveway that leads beyond her house to a separate two-car garage, she slows down. She not only slows her driving, but she also slows her mind so she can communicate everything that happened in town to her husband. They may not go back into town for a while. She needs Tom to understand all that she saw. She also doesn't want to freak out her son, who has already been having some issues. The last thing he needs is to see his mother in the throes of panic.

She pulls into the driveway and sees the two men in her life standing on the front porch. She pulls even with them and thinks again of the need to appear very calm right now. Turning off the Outback and opening her car door, she gets out and forces a smile. She knows Tom can tell something isn't right. Since she had gone through the anxiety issues and depression she experienced, Tom has developed a way of squinting his eyes when he looks at her. He can sense something isn't right. It's a look of inspection that she finds irritating. When he looks at her like this, it is because something is not right. His ability to know there is something off with her bothers her, not because she wishes to keep secrets, but because she can't see the same issues in Tom.

"Is that fog in town, honey? We heard the emergency sirens and walked down the driveway to see what was going on when we saw fog over the town. I also tried calling you, but the call didn't go through."

Sandy opens her mouth to answer when Bobby cuts her off, "Mom, what's wrong? You have a weird look on your face." Sandy isn't surprised that she can't completely conceal her emotions and her fear she feels but she again tries to be reassuring for her son. She forces a brief laugh, "Oh no Bobby, I'm just getting a little headache. Could you do me a favor and head inside so I can talk to your dad for a moment? I saw some birthday ideas for you in town and I want to tell daddy before I forget."

She can see Bobby is suspicious, but the potential for a great birthday gift is enough to motivate him to go inside. "Ok mom. Is it cool?"

Sandy laughs and this time it is genuine, "The coolest ever."

Bobby jumps up pumping his arms in the air and runs through the front door.

"I'm guessing you don't want to talk about Bobby's birthday. What's going on in Wray?"

"Oh my God, Tom! It's terrible. I am sure that Ruth Hilsers is dead, and the fog was so strange and I almost…" Tom interrupts his wife by taking her shaking shoulders in his hands, "Honey wait, slow down. One thing at a time. Ruth is dead?" Tom now looks genuinely upset and Sandy realizes she needs to slow down.

"Ok," she steps away from Tom's embrace, "I was at Sanders, I grabbed everything we needed and was at the register when I noticed that something seemed a little off outside. I asked Mr. Sanders if he thought so too and he told me it was getting dark too fast."

"Getting dark? It's only beginning to get dark now." Tom motions to the sky above them.

"Yes, here. But not in town. It was getting dark in Wray and as soon as Mr. Sanders pointed it out, I knew he was right. The fading light was what I had noticed but couldn't figure out."

Tom looks curiously at her, but not to show disbelief, and Sandy thinks Gin that Tom also knows something is wrong.

Sandy continues, "So I paid for our supplies and by the time I got to the doors to leave, it had gone dark and foggy."

"That fast?" Tom looks puzzled.

"Yes, that fast. Listen to me Tom, ok? You're going to make me forget something and I don't want to forget anything because we're in trouble here."

"Ok, sorry hon go ahead."

Sandy notes the wrinkles are back on Tom's forehead. "So, I went out to load the car and Tom the fog was so thick, and it smelled like something died in it. It stinks like decay. And while I was putting the stuff in the car, someone was out there with me, but I couldn't see them, I felt them twice and they even brushed against the back of me." As Sandy is recounting to Tom what had happened in the fog, she reaches back to her leg where she felt someone touch her. As Tom follows her hand, he puts a finger up and she stops talking.

74

"Sorry to interrupt Babe, but where did you feel something bump into you exactly?"

Sandy reaches back touching the back of her leg. When she feels the rough edges of torn material, she realizes why Tom stopped her. "Tom, what's wrong with my jeans here?"

"It looks like they've been cut."

Sandy knows her jeans were not cut or disturbed in any way when she put them on in the morning. In fact, she's only worn them twice before today. "These jeans are new, and they weren't torn up before." She looks at Tom, "Can you check my leg?"

Tom bends down and pulls the fabric apart. "Your leg is fine, but these jeans have a gash in them about 4 inches long Sands. You better finish telling me what happened in town."

Sandy is stunned that her jeans are torn, and Tom tries to get her started again, "Someone touched you where your jeans are cut and then what happened?"

"I felt something touch me and I panicked and jumped in the car to drive home. But on my way, I saw Ruth walking in the middle of the road.

I had seen her walking home on my way into town, so it surprised me to see her out walking in the fog. Tom, she was shell-shocked and bleeding from her head. She walked to my car and was talking to me through my window like she couldn't tell it was closed. That was when the town siren had gone on and I had to roll the window down to hear her. The fog was all around us and I couldn't understand much other than a man wouldn't let her get into her house. He had hit her, and she was so angry, she kept getting louder and louder, yelling about him hitting her. I kept thinking she needed to be quiet, so that whoever was in the fog wouldn't hear her. Apparently, a man hit her in the past and the fact that a man hit her today had her so pissed. I kept telling her to get in the car and finally she snapped out of it and agreed to get in the car. She walked around the back of the car but never came around to the passenger side and, oh Tom, it was terrible."

Tom can see Sandy is on the verge of tears and needs her to keep it together long enough to finish telling him what happened. Watching Sandy, he knows whatever happened is terrible. Bad enough that he needs to warn their neighbors up the road. "What happened next Sands?"

"She never came back to the car. She walked behind the car and then was gone." Sandy shudders remembering the feeling that she had sat motionless in the car surrounded by fog, "I finally decided I couldn't leave her out there so I started to get out of the car when someone reached for me out of the fog."

"Wait, what do you mean someone reached for you? Who was it?" Tom imagines one of the town drunks hassling his wife and feels his anger rising.

"I only saw a hand, but it was strange." Sandy's gaze drifts up to the right as she tries to remember that moment. "It had long fingers and looked old, like dark and weathered. OH! And the nails were SO long. It hit the outside of the car door and the sound it made!" She spins around so fast Tom for a moment thinks she's going to take off running, but she points to the Outback. Tom walks over and looks at the car door and can't come up with a reasonable explanation for what he sees. There are four gouges in the metal, deep tracks that run for three inches in a downward arch toward the handle, and they have deeply punctured the door.

"Sandy look at this. Are you telling me that someone's nails did this? To metal?"

Sandy looks at her husband and quietly says, "Yes I am, and you haven't heard what happened to

77

Ruth yet. Once you do, this…" She points at the damaged door, "will not seem very strange."

12

Steve and Sabrina Sellers had lived just outside of Wray, Colorado their entire lives. Being the same age, they had known each other through school, had been high school sweethearts and had married right after high school. The house they lived in on Highway 385, a couple of miles north of Wray, was the same house that had seen their children grow into adults. They had always been happy living here on the plains of Colorado, and it had never crossed either of their minds to live anywhere else. The people of Wray were the people they had grown up with, and they considered them a part of their extended family. Even newcomers like the Benton's seamlessly fit into the community. Steve and Sabrina often marveled at how Wray always seemed to draw the right kinds of people. The people of Wray were hard-working people. They respected each other's successes and were there to lend a helping hand when tragedy struck. A year before, when old man Smith's barn had burned to the ground in a heating oil accident, Steve had been right there with many other neighbors working day after day for a week until they built a new barn. Everyone involved made sure that the new barn was a vast improvement over the old one.

The locally owned lumber yard had donated the materials, and the community had donated their labor. It was something to see an old man who thought he was headed for an early retirement reduced to joyful tears when his neighbors had constructed the new barn.

Steve Sellers thought that you couldn't find that kind of community partnership in cities where everyone was out for themselves. In the cities, everything was a constant competition, with people treading all over each other in their never-ending attempts to get ahead. Of course, small-town living also meant everyone knew everyone, and that could lead to some gossip. Early in his marriage, Doris Weathers, town busy body that she was, had caused him trouble in his marriage. She had told his young wife that he spent too much time chatting up Valerie Short when she saw the two of them in the market. This had become quite the sore spot with Sabrina, who had always been a little jealous of the attention Valerie gave Steve. He had gotten to the point that when he saw Valerie in town that he would stay out of sight. Sabrina had thought he was up to no good with Valerie, but the issue had ultimately been resolved when Valerie married a mutual friend, John Smythe, and had moved away. The truth that he would never admit to his wife was that he found Valerie attractive, and Valerie had always been very flirtatious with him. While those things were true, he had never cheated on his wife and he never would. Admitting to Sabrina that he found Valerie attractive though would have caused even more trouble in his marriage. So, he had done what he thought was smart, and insisted that Valerie wasn't the slightest bit attractive to him. Doris had caused him a lot of trouble, and he had never spoken to the old bitty again. She had passed away several years ago, and he also skipped the funeral. He had decided there wasn't any reason to pretend he liked her because she had died.

"Penny for your thoughts, old man," Sabrina says to Steve as she finishes dropping the pasta she is making for dinner into a pot of boiling water on the stove. "You look deep in thought."

Steve finishes kicking off his work boots and enters the kitchen. The room has yellow walls and white tile floors. It is dated, but many delicious meals continued to be made here. "Oh, I was thinking about how lucky we are." All these years later he still isn't crazy enough to invoke the name of Valerie Short with his wife.

"Yes, we are, I couldn't agree more. And you are lucky because your wife is making a great new recipe tonight." She smiles at her husband, who is a creature of habit and doesn't particularly like surprises, especially in his diet. This news gets Steve's attention, and he wanders toward the stove to see what she is making. "Now, you get out of here. You'll like it and it sure isn't poisoned, so even if you don't, you'll live through the experience of trying something new."

"Yes, ma'am," Steve tells his wife. He knows better after thirty-five years than to argue with her. He's pretty sure in all their years together he hasn't won an argument yet. Sabrina had a strong will, and it was that part of her that kept him in line and kept them together. "I thought about putting the clippers to the front hedge today but ran out of time, so I'll get on that tomorrow."

Steve says this to his wife, but mostly to himself as an affirmation that he will take care of the chore tomorrow. If it was up to him, he'd have long ago pulled the hedge out of the ground, but Sabrina had always loved it.

"Well, it's about time. I was getting ready to tell you that hedge won't trim itself." Sabrina laughs, and it is a sound that has always made Steve feel that all is right in the world. Without that laugh in his home, nothing would have been right.

"We have something strange going on today. I thought about calling up Tom to see what he could see down in Wray." Steve says this to his wife as she is stirring something that he admits smells good.

"What is it?"

Steve replies to his wife, "Looks like fog."

Sabrina laughs, "Old man if you're seeing fog on a July evening, I'm thinking we need to get you in to see Doc Alders." It has always amused him she called him an old man because they are the same age.

"Ha. Ha. Ha. You are hilarious, but I'm serious. There is a bank of what looks like a fog hanging over Wray. You can't even see the town. I'm going to call Tom up and see if he can see anything since they're so much closer than we are."

Sabrina shrugs this off and wonders what her husband had been doing outside. Whatever he saw, a fog bank made no sense. Steve gets up, putting a hand on his lower back, and grumbles something about aging being a wicked thing and gimps to the phone hanging on the kitchen wall. He dials Tom Benton and waits for a minute before declaring, "That's odd, nothing."

"Nothing?" Sabrina looks at Steve, raising her eyebrows in curiosity.

"There's no dial tone."

Sabrina shakes her head, "Well if you weren't so dang stubborn you'd get us a cell phone like the rest of the world instead of relying on that old landline, which seems to have more and more troubles as time goes by. It's not safe. At our age, we should have a phone we can rely on."

"Yeah, when the world ends all that technology is going to go with it. We will have our phone here and everyone else will be shit outta luck." Steve says this with a sense of satisfaction and smiles.

"Well super genius husband of mine, since we are the only people left in the world with a landline phone, we would be as shit outta luck as everyone else because even if that thing still worked, we'd have no one to call."

Steve laughs at this because she's right, but also because he has always loved his wife's quick wit. He looks around the kitchen and for the tenth time in the last month thinks the room needs some updating. Many of the rooms in the old farmhouse had been updated and modernized, but not this room. This kitchen had been like this since their children had been little, which now that he thought about it was probably why Sabrina refused to allow him to at least paint it. She was a woman of tradition and it had been very hard on her to become an empty nester. Steve glances at the curtains on the window by the back door. He bets himself that he could at least talk Sabrina into changing these when something he sees outside causes him to take a second glance.

"What the heck?" He walks to the window and looks out between the curtains. He sees gray swirls of condensation and nothing else.

"What is it? Tell me my garden didn't get torn up by those dang rabbits again."

"No, it's not that, but it would appear you can cancel my trip to see the doc. We got ourselves fog." Steve parts the curtains further so his wife can see the window.

"Well......" Sabrina is stumped, "I can't believe it. In the middle of July, no less. I've never seen that before."

13

Tom runs a finger over the gouge in the car door and says to Sandy, "Tell me what happened to Ruth."

Sandy hesitates. She's not sure how to say this so that Tom won't think she's crazy. "Listen, I know this is a lot," She motions at the car and then down to her jeans, "So I don't want you to think I'm losing it." After saying this, she taps her head. "When I saw that hand, I got the door shut, and I started driving immediately, and as I did….."

Tom waits, and looks at his wife with concern, but not because he doesn't believe her. Sandy begins again, "Ruth fell straight out of the air and landed next to me on the road. She was…her body was so mangled that I only know it was her because I could see one leg sticking up in the air. She had her white stockings on, and I could see it and Tom. There was blood all over it. I could swear I heard something too." Sandy inspects Tom's expression. What she sees reassures her he doesn't think she's crazy, "I am almost sure that I heard something in the air, like wings. Wings flapping and flying."

Now that it was out, she felt relief whether or not he believed her, but she can tell that he does. "I'm not sure what made that sound, and I'm not sure what is going on in Wray. Maybe there are other people there who are hurt, or maybe everyone is fine, but it is so strange to have fog at this time of year and I can't explain everything that happened because it makes no sense but it all happened just the same. And that hand......" She gathers her thoughts and then says, "How did Ruth fall from the air? And the fog, it smelled rotten."

Tom pulls out his cell phone again and dials Steve and Sabrina. He waits and gets the now familiar tone is his ear. The call will not go through. "This is the same thing that happened when I tried to call you. Calls aren't working." He walks back down the driveway, pauses, and turns back to Sandy. "Honey, park the car in the garage, I'm going to look up the road at Steve's place."

"Okay, but hold on a second." Sandy reaches in the car and pulls out her cell phone. She dials their neighbors' number, grumbles to herself, and then tries calling Tom's cell phone. She looks at Tom, "The same thing, it's not working. After I put the car away I'm going inside to find Bobby. But what are we going to do? And what will we tell Bobby? And how can we get a hold of the Sherriff to tell him about Ruth? And then, what if he doesn't believe me?"

"Sands, one thing at a time. We can't do anything about the phones and we sure aren't driving back there into the fog. I'll go look and see what I can see and then I'll come back inside with you and we will figure out what to do."

He hesitates and Sandy calls him out on it, "What? Say it."

"While you were gone, I had cranked up the handheld radio. I could hear someone, but not very well. A man. He was saying that someone wanted in his house and that he wasn't sure how many of them there were. I thought it was a joke. Now I'm not so sure." As Tom looks at her, Sandy knows he is about to tell her something worse, "And Sands, I spoke with Bobby. He says that when he saw the man in his window, there was fog."

Sandy turns away without saying a word and gets in the car. She doesn't want Tom to see the tears that threaten to let loose and she doesn't want him to hear her voice begin to waver.

14

Mearl Roal (pronounced like roll) was not a kind man, and no one knew this more than his son. Mearl had solid control over all things in the Roal household, which in the past had included his wife. She knew the backside of Mearl's hand like she knew her image in the mirror. For Mearl's son, the introduction to the creative abuses Mearl leveled on those he controlled began at birth. His father named his son Cinnamon and nicknamed him Sin for short. Sin was always told that this was in his best interest because it was a tough world and he needed to be tougher. As a young child Sin never wanted to admit his given name was Cinnamon, and even though he wasn't crazy about Sin, it garnered him much less attention than Cinnamon. Now, in his seventeenth year of life, he still hated both of his names almost as much as he hated his father. His father's goal had been to make Sin into 'one tough S.O.B.' An S.O.B. that the long line of abusive Roal men could be proud of, however, there was a problem with this as Sin wasn't a chip off his fathers' block. He was nothing like the drunken, ill-tempered Mearl. Sin appreciated creativity, nature, and peace. Sin's mother often told to him that his father was insecure around him because Sin was smarter than both of his parents put together. Sin knew his intelligence was high, at least higher than that of his father, but he never wanted that to show around Mearl for fear of what Mearl might do to him.

When Sin had failed his father's first attempt at teaching him to hunt, he had cried only slightly more tears for the rabbit he had killed than he had the beating he had taken for crying over the rabbit. This had been the last time his mother had tried to intervene in his father's discipline measures with Sin because Mearl had given his mother twice what he had given Sin. Mearl had later told Sin, "Your momma got a mouth on her and it ain't near purty enough to listen to. People with a gash between their legs need to mind their position in life when it comes to those who don't got no gash, and she's gonna learn that lesson."

It seemed that Sin's mom did learn a lesson of some sort, although it wasn't the lesson Mearl intended, because, within a week of that beating, she had left for good. It had been seven years now, and Sin had not seen his mother again. When Sin had finally gathered the nerve to ask Mearl why his mom hadn't been home for a week Mearl had only told Sin (after attempting a drunken punch at Sin's face) that she had gone and runoff and "fuck her", neither of them needed her. Sin had sure felt like he had needed her. He spent two weeks reeling and grieving this loss. At every sound of a car approaching the mobile home they lived in at the edge of Mearl's auto salvage yard, hope would spring inside Sin. The young Sin imagined his mother finally returning home to rescue him from his abusive father. That hope always died a painful death, as time after time it was a customer, not his mother. After the first couple of weeks of sadness over the disappearance of his mom, Sin had grown a strong resentment toward her for leaving him alone with the same devil she had run from. And as his father had so eloquently stated, fuck her for leaving him.

After his mother had abandoned him to the whims and abuses of Mearl, things had gotten much worse for Sin. One night when Mearl had drunk enough to black out on the living room couch, Sin had gone to meet his only friend, Rita. She was his friend and if he got his way, she would become more. She wasn't the pretty princess type of girl, and that was why he liked her. Instead of makeup and dresses, she was all blue jeans and tomboy. He loved hanging out with Rita but made sure he didn't stay gone too long. It terrified him for Mearl to find out about Rita. He had been gone an hour and felt sure that Mearl would never know. As his luck would have it, someone from Wray had come to the salvage yard looking for an alternator for a 2001 Ford Taurus. The customer had woken Mearl up from his drunken slumber. When Sin had come home Mearl had explained through gritted teeth and very slurred words that Sin was as useful as a limp dick at a porn convention and while Sin had been out running around (more than a whole team of Kenyan's) Mearl had to wait on the customers that Sin had been neglecting. On and on the lecture went, even though it had only been one customer and Mearl didn't have the Ford part in his inventory, anyway. As Mearl had stood up from his chair and removed his belt (always the precursor to a beating) Sin did the only thing he could think of to save himself. He told Mearl that he had been out with a girl. Mearl had frozen with his belt halfway out of the belt loops on his pants and stared dumbfounded at Sin.

"Bullshit." Mearl had said, but Sin noticed the lack of conviction in Mearl's voice.. "If you was out with a girl, whass her name?"

Sin had no trouble after his years of living with Mearl, deciphering his dad's drunk speech.

"Rita." Sin knew he had opened a can of worms he had not wanted to open, but it kept the belt and the fists from flying in his direction.

"What was you doin with Reeeetah?" Mearl drew out Rita's name sarcastically showing he didn't believe in the mythical Rita. However, Sin could see the hope lingering in his father's expression.

"We were just out walking and talking, but I was with her because I like her... a little." And there it was. The horse had come out of the barn and Mearl had completely changed his tone.

"Well, I'll be damned. Boy, I figured you was goin to end up shootin hoops for the other team. I didn't figure you was too interested in whass under skirts." Mearl had flopped back down on the couch and had passed out again. Sin had remained only slightly hopeful that the conversation would disappear in the alcoholic cloud of Mearl's mind, but the next day Mearl was in a chipper mood and was treating Sin better than he ever had.

Mearl had offered Sin money to go into town and grab them some burgers from the A & W, which he never did. When Sin had returned with their lunch Mearl sat across the kitchen table from Sin with a grin a mile wide.

"You got a picture of this Rita?" When Mearl had asked this question, Sin knew it was either show Mearl one of the photos of Rita on his phone or suffer the consequences of his father's doubts. He reluctantly pulled his phone out and held up the screen. In the picture, Rita was laughing at him and getting ready to throw a pen at him for disturbing her homework. He had taken the photo spur of the moment and it was one of his favorite pictures of her.

Mearl studied the photo for a moment as though making an important decision and then looked to his son, "Well I won't exactly be bragging to the boys about you nailing any high-quality tail but yeah, she'll do fine. You get any yet?"

"Dad, no, I mean .."

"Well, don't you worry about it. That one looks like she was built for breedin, you'll get a piece. Just slip a cover on it. We don't need no buns in the oven around here, you understand?"

"Yes, sir." Sin hated his father as much as he ever had at that moment, but this was much better than getting a 'correctin' as his dad often had described the physical punishments he doled out.

Mearl accepted that answer and continued, "I was thinking you would end up playing the skin flute, so this is good news! Calls for a bit of a celebration. You bring that girl around here so your old man can give her the once over. Invite her over

for some steaks and beers. I'll fire up the grill."
Mearl smiled at Sin as though he had extended a
very kind offer, but Sin cringed inside. Shit, he had
thought, the last thing he needed was Rita over
around Mearl. Especially if Mearl was drinking.

Now, a week later, and after plenty of
excuse-making, Sin knew time was running out on
Mearl's patience. He was going to have to cave in
and bring Rita over, which also meant he was going
to have to explain a little about his father. His
stomach hurt every time he imagined how rude
Mearl would end up being to Rita, and oh God,
once the drinking began, he would have to get Rita
home. Sin was sitting in the living room staring at
the TV, but oblivious to whatever was on. Mearl
was in the kitchen slamming dishes around and
cussing about something. Sin was about to ask if he
needed help when he realized he needed to turn on
some lights inside the trailer. It was getting very
dark. Maybe a storm would come through and tear
up something on their property, and Mearl would
have something else to focus on other than Rita. Sin
switches on the lamp beside him and then peers out
the living room window. It puzzles him to see that
has fog completely enveloped them. Weird, he
thinks, it had been a bright day just twenty minutes
ago.

15

"I'm guessing you liked dinner since you had two big plates." Sabrina Sellers raises her eyebrows at her husband as she says this to him.

"I have to admit, this is now a favorite of mine." Steve shovels in the last bite of dinner he scraped together on his plate and leans back in his chair, stuffed.

"Good, I'm glad you liked it, and I'm glad you can admit it." She winks at her husband and stands up to clear the dishes from the table when they hear the unmistakable sound of the doorbell. "How would anyone find their way out here in that fog bank?" Sabrina watches as Steve makes his way to the living room and the front door of their home.

As she stacks dishes into the kitchen sink, a thought pops into her head. Strange that I should think of Valerie Short after all these years. No doubt it had been a blessing that woman had married and moved away. Continuing to work on the dishes, she rubs at her temple, smearing tomato sauce on the side of her head.

She hadn't thought about the situation involving Valerie in a very long time, but now that she had, she was having a hard time not being angry. She could feel the same feeling she had those many years ago. Distrust. She didn't enjoy looking at her husband and seeing someone devious, someone she didn't know, which is exactly what happened back then. In fact, she hadn't been sure that their marriage would survive. Did Valerie kiss Steve back then? Was that something that had happened, or was that something that her imagination had created? She couldn't remember if Steve had been cheating or not, but it seemed like a lot more happened back then than kissing.

"Oh, my lord. Forget it and get moving." Sabrina says this to herself when she realizes that she has lost track of how long she has been standing at the kitchen sink. She feels some lingering anger at Steve when she remembers he had gone into the living room because the doorbell rang. "Steve, who's at the door?"

Steve returns to the kitchen and when she sees him, she wants to reach out and slap him. How had she forgiven a man who cheated on her? Not only that, she had stayed with him and had children with him. Was she crazy?

"Are you okay Sabrina? You look a little lost." Steve is staring at her with an empty look. She wants to scream in his face that she would be a lot better if he hadn't been out whoring around with that God damn Valerie Short, although there had been nothing short about her with those long legs that men all across town ogled. No, she wonders for a second if she's having a stroke because she now remembers Steve hadn't cheated on her at all. Nothing had happened other than her jealousy. Steve had even gone out of his way to avoid Valerie to reassure Sabrina that he had no interest in her.

"No, I'm fine, wondering who was ringing our bell."

"Well, strangest thing. I can't see anyone out there through the peephole."

"So no one is there….." The doorbell rings again, and it startles them both.

"Well, dammit." Steve again heads into the living room and this time Sabrina follows him.

"Steve, don't open the door, just look through the peephole," Sabrina says this to Steve as she parts the curtains next to the front door to look out the window. She sees no one on the front porch.

"No one there unless they're a little kid or someone short."

Sabrina wonders to herself why he would bring up Valerie's maiden name. It takes her a moment to realize Steve isn't talking about Valerie.

"Okay," she tells Steve, "Step back from the door and come over by me." She closes the curtains. "Let's stand here for a moment and see if the bell rings again. We'll catch whoever is messing with us."

She has a determined look as she steps in front of the window. Steve stands beside his wife, waiting. They are both standing silently, and it doesn't even take a full minute before the bell rings again. Steve jumps to the peephole in the door as his wife opens the curtains over the window.

Sabrina is shocked by who she sees standing on their front porch. "Are you kidding me? What the hell is she doing here?"

"She?" Steve is puzzled, "It's a man, and he stepped back into the fog. I saw him moving back from the door."

"No, get over here and look at your precious girlfriend." Steve sees the color in his wife's cheeks and knows she is angry. Looking out the window, Steve sees no one. He looks to Sabrina and back out the window.

"Sabrina, I'm not sure who you're talking about, but the porch is empty. There was a man there, and he stepped off the porch."

How big a liar her husband of so many years has become. "Steven, you look right there at Valerie Short standing on our porch waiting for you and you have the nerve to tell me there is no one there? How damn long has this been going on?"

"Sabrina, what in Sam Hill's name are you going on about. There is not one person on our porch, let alone Valerie Short."

"Alright, let's open the door and talk to this figment of my imagination, shall we?" Sabrina moves to the door and Steve grabs her by the arm.

"No! I have a bad feeling about this. The fog, the man, you are seeing things that aren't there. I haven't seen Valerie since you have, it's been thirty years and there is no one on our porch. Don't open that door."

"Oh, how convenient. We'll stand here pretending that she isn't out there on our porch until she leaves, and then you can go on screwing her when I'm not looking. Well, you listen to me and you listen good, there is no way I'm just standing here while she comes to my house and flaunts her affair with my husband."

"What is wrong with you?" Steve can't believe what he is hearing. He looks out the window again at the empty front porch. There is no one on the outside, and he very clearly saw the shape of a man in a long overcoat retreating from the porch only moments ago. "Sabrina, something isn't right here but I am telling you, we need to get you sat down because you're seeing things and I'm worried you aren't well. No one is out there. No one."

"Let go of my arm and MOVE it!"

Steve has never seen his wife so angry and he lets go of her arm. He reasons maybe it's best she opens the door to see no one on the porch. Then he might convince her to come to sit down. Damn that phone not working. He should already be calling an ambulance. Shit, now I'll end up getting a cell phone for sure, he thinks.

Sabrina throws open the door and raises a pointing finger to the person she expects to be on the porch when she stops and for the first time loses the look of conviction on her face.

"Where the hell did she go? She was just here." She peers beyond the porch into the fog. "Valerie Short, you get your ass back here and we will have ourselves a chat you little home-wrecking hussy!" With that, Sabrina steps across the threshold. Steve can see the fabric on her sleeve ripple as she lets her arm fall back to her side. He knows in that instant she is in terrible danger, and he reaches toward his departing wife to pull her back inside their house.

"Sabrina NO!" Steve gets two fingers on the sleeve of her blouse when something that feels like fire digs into his arm. He screams out in warning to Sabrina and looks to see what has dug into the flesh on his left forearm. A hand. His blood pours over the fingers that have pierced his skin. He looks to Sabrina and wonders why she is moving backward. It seems strange to him she would be drifting back toward the open front door when her legs aren't moving. That's when he realizes that Sabrina is not moving backward, in fact, she is not moving at all. She seems to have frozen in place with a horrified look as she gazes at what has grabbed his arm. No, Sabrina is not moving backward, I am moving forward Steve thinks, I am being pulled into the fog.

16

Tom reaches the edge of the blacktop highway at the end of his driveway. He is afraid to look to his left toward Wray, so instead, he looks to his right toward his neighbors, Steve and Sabrina's home. He thinks since the phones aren't working, he should drive on up to their place and at least give them some warning about what Sands experienced in town. When he looks to the north, he cannot see their home. Instead, he sees the gray swirling mist of fog. He looks back to his left and sees that the fog has grown about halfway between Wray and his own home. The fog is expanding and somehow has wrapped around to the north and has enshrouded the Seller's place.

Tom knows that it is only a matter of time before the fog reaches his place. He knows that it is becoming very important to figure out a plan. There may be no emergency at all and there could be a rational explanation for what is happening in Wray, but he can't gamble on that possibility. Within a few moments it will be dark. He needs to prepare for the worst-case scenario. When he thinks about his wife's description of what happened to Ruth Hilsers, he is baffled to come up with a reasonable explanation. To Tom, the worst case is that they need to board up windows and prepare for whatever shredded his wife's jeans and gouged holes in the Outback's side. That is going to be a very tall task. He does not understand what they could potentially be dealing with, but there are just too many coincidences with what Bobby has seen the past few nights and what Sands described to him. It doesn't seem possible, and yet here they are, he thinks.

Without another glance at the fog bank that he knows is rapidly approaching his own home, he turns and begins walking back to the house. As he does this, the unmistakable popping sound of gunfire can be heard coming from the direction of town. He stops walking and turns his head to the south, toward town, and listens as more gunfire erupts. He feels a sense of impending doom. There is something in that fog bank and it is coming for them. It is coming, and it is coming quickly.

17

Sin isn't sure why he didn't hear his father coming up behind him, but he had been lost in thought, staring out the living room window at the fog. The fog was thick looking and as he watches he notices how it swirls as though something is moving within that he can't see. It is also growing darker, almost by the second.

"You gonna come eat or stand there jerkin off at the window all day? Better save some of that action for Rita." Mearl laughs at his creative humor and then realizes his son is captivated by something outside. "What are you looking at?"

"Fog."

"Fog? How we got us a fog this time a year?" Mearl, stepping a little unsteady brushes Sin out of his way and stares out the window. "Well, I'll be a frog's ass. Sure nuff."

"It looks like something is out there causing that fog to move. Like it swirls around from time to time." Sin looks at the side of his dad's face, waiting for his thoughts.

"You watch too many of them hoar movies. Ain't nothin out there other than a bunch of fog." Mearl snorts this at his son and closes the window curtain. "Let's go eat, boy."

The doorbell rings as Sin and Mearl sit down to the chili that Mearl has heated from a can and they stop looking at the food to look at each other. "Well, go on and get the door. Could be a customer."

Standing up from the table, Sin thinks it would be a little strange for a customer to drive out to their salvage yard in such a thick fog. It was getting so dark outside, but the doorbell rang, and no one stopped by here unless they were coming for car parts. Sin pulls the curtain aside from the living room window next to the front door and peers out at the concrete pad in front of the door. There is no one there. He closes the window and next looks through the peephole in the front door. No one there at all. Strange, he thinks. Maybe the doorbell has a short in it.

Returning to the dining room table, Sin says, "No one was there." He knows this will get a reaction from his father.

"If there ain't no one there, someone is messing with us and that means that someone has an

107

ass kickin a comin," Mearl says this as he tries to take a bite from his bowl of chili. Sauce spills from his spoon, down his chin and on the front of his shirt. He doesn't know this has happened, which is usually a good sign he is already drunk.

"Maybe there's an electrical short in the doorbell. Seems strange someone would come out here in that fog." Sin says this aloud, but mainly to himself.

"Well, wouldn't surprise me the way everything around here is a fallin apart. God damn mother of yours cost me a fortune, leaving us in the lurch the way she did. Hard to keep up with all the finances now. But a bitch is always a bitch. Don't forget that now that you is messin with the fairer sex."

Sin has no idea how his mother's leaving could have affected them financially as Mearl has insisted many times over, but he does not express these thoughts as he is almost sure they would lead to Mearl's temper and a 'correctin' he wants nothing to do with.

"Now, with this Rita you want to get your paws on.." Mearl's thoughts often drift when he is drinking, and he sometimes has a hard time finishing one thought before the next arrives, "Oh and when

is this Rita going to accept my invitation for …."
The doorbell rings again. Mearl grinds his teeth,
"See? It's no short in the doorbell, it's some kids
messin with us. Probably them dumb fuckin Wells
kids from down the road. Pains in the ass they are
wouldn't surprise me. I'll check this time. We will
have to wait them out. Let's fuck with 'em a bit.
Will serve em right. Come with me. You look out
the window, but real slight so they can't see you and
I'll look through the peephole. When they come up
to the door, the next time I'll jump out and give
them a little of what those shits deserve. A little
Mearlness."

A little 'Mearlness' was one of his father's
many made-up catchphrases. It was Mearl speak for
meanness. Mearl temporarily looks as though he will
trip leaving the table and fall, but he finds his step
and heads for the front door. Sin knows his
participation is mandatory, so he follows his father to
the living room.

18

Sabrina leans against the inside of her front door and stares into her living room, shaking and shivering. Her body vibrates as though it is plugged into an electric wall socket, but she is unaware of her physical self. She sees the replay over and over of Steve being pulled out of her grasp into the fog by someone, something. It was a man, but he was different. She could see the man looking at her as he jerked her husband from her reach. He was so pale, and his features somehow old, so ancient and yet strong. He was shiny, like a plastic mannequin in the store, and yet he was real. His skin was so clear with such sheen on it. Something was wrong about him. He was real, and he wasn't. Under the surface, he was aged, very old. She had screamed her husband's name and saw the look of resignation on Steve's face. In that one look, she knew their life together was over. All the many years of raising kids, family barbeques, vacations, their minor arguments, and the lifelong love they shared were done. In an instant, it all was gone and the look on Steve's face said he thought they would have more time. It said he thought the ending would look much different. She had screamed his name and the shiny old man had laughed inside her mind. His mouth widened and opened in an impossibly enormous grin. When she saw the many pinpoint sharp teeth jutting from his mouth she had stumbled back inside their home and slammed the door.

A deep sob emerges from inside of her as she realizes it is all her fault. Why had she insisted on reliving the jealousy she had felt so many years ago over Valerie Short? She hadn't thought of her once in at least a decade before today. Her pathetic insecurities cost her the life of the only man she had ever loved. He was gone and with him the life and many years they had together. It had been so irrational to feel envy over someone who had not been a factor in their lives in so long. And why did she think she saw Valerie on her doorstep? It had seemed so real but, Valerie had not been here. At all. She had hallucinated her. Steve had tried telling her that Valerie wasn't outside. Now that she considerrd the moment that Valerie seemed to stand outside, it made no sense. Valerie had appeared the same as the last time she had seen her. She looked like she was twenty-one years of age. Valerie may have been a very attractive woman, but everyone aged. This many years later there was no way Valerie could look twenty-one, no way.

Sabrina.

Her name is uttered within the confines of her mind, not within the living room where she crouches by the front door. She realizes she is shivering. She is afraid to respond to the voice and afraid not to respond. It is the man who had her husband, and she is scared, even more scared for Steve than herself.

"Y...yes?" Sabrina says this aloud in her living room and then holds her breath waiting to see if she will hear the old man again.

As you know, I have your husband. If you come outside, the two of you can be together. Come out.

"Don't hurt him!" Sabrina screams this at the man, who she knows is on the other side of the door she.

Then come out.

"How do I know you will do as you say?"

Oh, Sabrina, you are delightful. You don't know if I will keep my word or not. But if you love your husband, and I believe you do, you will come out. Wouldn't you like to be with him?

Sabrina contemplates what the old man says to her. She wants to be with Steve. She needs Steve. Maybe if she complies with the old man's request, she and Steve will get through this and return to their normal lives. The old man probably wants to steal from their home. If she gives him what he wants, he can take anything he desires and leave.

"Do you promise?"

Promise what, Sabrina?

Sabrina feels the beginning of hope, "Do you promise I can be with Steve and you won't hurt him?"

The old man chuckles at this.

Of course, I promise. My word is my currency.

"Okay, I'll come out. But you promise, right? You can take whatever you want. I just want to be with Steve."

Yes, as I said. And I usually take what I need. Want only plays a small part in it.

Sabrina stands up, her back against the door, and says a silent prayer. Please lord, she thinks, help me to be making the right decision. She pivots to face the door and turns the handle. She opens the door and sees the shape of the man moving through the fog toward her. When he is close enough to see his features, she again thinks he is much older than he looks. There is something about his appearance. It is as though he has been chiseled from stone. The angles of his nose and jaw are sharp, and his skin shines as though he has a layer of jell rubbed across his face. His eyes are big. They are large orbs within his skull, and they are entirely black.

He reaches out his hand to her.

Let's go see Steve.

Sabrina swallows the lump she feels in her throat and places her hand within his grasp. It is cold and dry, like leather in winter. She feels his large hand fold over hers and the strength she feels in his grip amazes her. He is incredibly strong. She can feel a slight pinch on the back of her hand as his protruding nails brush her skin. If he wanted, he could crush her hand. She tries looking away but cannot. He holds her gaze as they move further into the fog. She notices the smell in the fog. Death and rotting. Her pulse increases.

"Where is Steve?"

He is right here. But first Sabrina, tell me about your friend, Sandy.

This catches Sabrina off guard, "Sandy? Sandy Benton?"

Yes, your friend up the road.

"Is that what this is about? What has she done? She's a good friend and so kind. If she did something wrong, I'm sure she wouldn't have meant to."

No Sabrina, she has done nothing wrong; I wish to get to know her a little.

The old man gives her hand a squeeze, indicating he would indeed like to hear her speak about Sandy.

"Well, I'm a little unsure of where to begin," Sabrina hesitates, "You're taking me to Steve?"

Yes, I am.

As they move, Sabrina knows she is walking, and he is moving with her, but his legs are not moving. His feet do not appear to be touching the ground. This is most worrisome to her, but she knows she must keep speaking.

"Well, she is our neighbor, and she is very kind. We just adore her son Bobby and oh, her husband, Tom, he and Steve get along famously. They're good neighbors and friends. Almost family."

Do you believe they feel the same affection for you?

She thinks this is a strange question but agrees. "Yes, they like us as much as we like them."

Do you believe that the Benton's would want to protect you from harm?

Sabrina thinks this is a very concerning question and does not like what it implies. "Yes, of course, they would, they're our friends."

That is most excellent Sabrina. One more question.

He stops their forward momentum and turns her to face him.

Do you believe Sandy and Tom to be strong people?

He sees the puzzled look on her face.

Strong intellectually.

"Oh yes, for sure. They're a strong, loving family. Strong character. Very devoted to one another. We treasure our friendship with them."

I thank you Sabrina for your candor.

The man turns from her and stares into the fog. Shortly, a figure appears. The figure also moves without moving its legs. It floats closer to them and she can see that it is a woman. The woman is too far to see perfectly, but Sabrina can see the feminine curves and knows she is female. The woman has something clutched in her right hand. It is large and somewhat round. Sabrina stares into the woman's face as she gets closer. She is aware that this woman has the same shine to her skin as the old man, but she is much younger than he, and she is beautiful. Like the old man, she is dressed in black. She is in a black top that is open enough to reveal white, milky skin and an ample bosom. The woman has a knowing, expectant grin that Sabrina does not like at all. She feels as though she and the old man know something that she does not. The fog swirls around the woman, caressing her like a lover and Sabrina cannot see below her waist.

117

Let us not keep the lovely Sabrina from the reunion with her beloved that I have promised.

The man is speaking to the woman who has appeared in front of Sabrina and for the first time, she notices that he speaks without opening his mouth. The woman's right arm moves upward and Sabrina cringes, expecting the woman to strike her. Instead, the woman holds an object before her. She is confused. This is what she noticed the woman carrying through the fog, but her mind cannot make sense of what she sees. She is looking into familiar eyes; They are distorted. They are green but dull. One eye is tilted, looking inward at the nose below it while the other eye, also dull and dry, stares straight at her. He is smiling. She is empty.

Realization settles as the woman laughs at her without opening her mouth. She has been looking into these eyes every day for the past several decades. The woman extends her arm closer to Sabrina and something wet splashes across her chest. She touches the front of her dress and feels a warm, thick liquid on her palm. Holding her hand between her and the face before her, she sees thickening blood. Beyond her hand is her husband's face. Finally, understanding clicks that the blood on her chest and her hand has come from Steve's neck, which is no longer attached to Steve's body. Thick, rubbery strands of red and blue dangle shredded from Steve's torn neck, and his mouth tilts in an unnatural angle. The grin on his face is because of a dislocated jaw and she can see the bulge on the right side of his face.

Sandy stumbles backward, but the old man holds her up. The laughter inside her mind is now both the woman and the old man. A scream erupts from the fog, "YOU PROMISED ME YOU FUCKING LIAR, YOU PROMISED!" Sabrina wonders who it is that is screaming until her mind clicks again and she knows it is she.

Yes, I did promise, and I have honored that promise, Sabrina. I promised you could be with Steve and here you are now with Steve.

Sabrina is now sobbing, and the energy that had erupted from her is gone, replaced with resignation and an awareness of her own death. The death of her sanity and the death of her spirit.

"You promised you wouldn't hurt him." I am dying, she thinks and vomits into the fog.

Well, Sabrina, I promised not to hurt him after I had already killed him. Promise kept, as it wasn't possible to hurt him anymore.

119

With that, the old man turns her away from Steve's dangling head and pulls her close to his face. She is aware that his breath contains the same smell of death that surrounds her in the fog. The smell overpowers the sour taste of puke in her mouth. His eyes somehow have become even darker and his grip on her shoulders hurts her. She feels the points of his nails digging into her shoulders and she wishes he would squeeze harder and end her. His mouth opens, and row after row of jagged, blood-drenched teeth protrude. His black tongue flicks across his teeth and blood, Steve's blood sprays a path across her cheek. The old man's jaw continues to extend lower, opening his mouth wide. Too wide. She thinks this should be impossible, but his jaw stretches lower and lower.

Looking up into his eyes, Sabrina is denied the only thing she wants now. Death.

You and I have some work to do. You can, and will be, very helpful soon. I would very much like to meet your lovely neighbors before this night ends and you will help make that happen.

The man throws her like she is nothing more than a rag doll across the stretch of ground between him and the woman. The woman snatches Sabrina out of the air and pulls her close. She recognizes the same smell of death emanating from the woman. The woman flicks her black tongue across her lips, and inside her mind, Sabrina hears the woman very clearly.

Let's go have some fun bitch.

With that Sabrina is swept up with the woman at an incredibly fast rate of speed into the swirling strands of fog above her in the dark sky.

19

Back inside the house, Tom sits at the dining table with his wife while Bobby is upstairs. He is lost deep in thought. Trying to make an educated guess about what is going on creates a battle with his rational mind.

"Sandy, we need to board up the windows," he sees the fear in her eyes, "The problem is the fog is moving so fast I don't think I can even get the lumber from the garage in time. Steve and Sabrina's place is covered in fog now as well as the town. And," Steve lowers his voice further, "while I was outside, I could hear gunfire. People are shooting at something in town. I think you got out of there just in time."

Sandy reacts to this news with a gasp and holds a hand to her heart, "Oh Tom, I hope Steve and Sabrina are okay. I'm not sure what happened in town, but it has something to do with the fog. We shouldn't even have fog on a summer afternoon. There is something in the fog and that is what …" She trails off as she relives her memories of being in town. "That's what got Ruth."

"I would be a little concerned hearing you say something like that, but I'm having a hard time explaining everything that happened to you in town. If you saw Ruth being murdered, then there is most definitely something in the fog. And that fog is coming here."

"You don't need to board up the windows."

Tom and Sandy both turn in their seats to see their son standing on the stairs behind them.

"Why is that Bobby?"

"Because the man at my window is the man who lives in the fog. And he can't come inside our house unless we let him in."

Tom glances at Sandy, who is looking at Bobby.

"Bobby, how do you know this?"

"Because what he wanted every night that he came here was for me to let him inside. He can't let himself in or he already would have done it. I don't even think he could see me through my window because his eyes never followed me when I ran from my room."

"Sandy, Bobby may be onto something. If he wanted in so badly, he probably would already have broke in, not demand Bobby let him in. And, if this man was at Bobby's second-floor window, and you saw," Tom hesitates with Bobby now listening, "well, you saw Ruth falling to the road, it would explain the sounds of flapping wings you heard."

Bobby looks at his parents and appreciates for the thousandth time that his parents love him and want to protect him. But he is tired of them treating him like a baby. He may not be grown up, but he is not a baby. "I heard what you said about Ruth. I'm not a baby. She's dead and if she fell out of the air. It is the scary man who I saw. I told you both. He was at my window and he wanted me to let him inside."

Tom says, "I'm going to run back out and see if the fog has slowed down. I believe what you're saying, Bobby, but it would make me feel better to board up our windows if I have enough time. We have a lot of supplies here and we have a gun." He pauses and as he leaves the room says to Sandy, "if we need it."

Tom walks out of the dining room and Sandy looks at her son. She can still see the little two-year-old kid who had been her constant companion. How he had loved being with her. As he aged the innocence of his youth was escaping. There was a little piece of her heart that hurt when she thought about that. Now that he was eight years old, he was becoming a young man and desired to spend more time with Tom than he did with her. That also hurt a little, but she continued to love him more every day. When she thought of what happened to Ruth. a deep fear settled over her and she couldn't afford to live in that fear. Not now with the fog approaching and so much unknown about what was happening in Wray.

"Bobby, why can't that scary man just break into our house since he wanted in so badly?"

"I'm not sure mom, but I don't think he can. But if I had opened the door or window for him, I don't think we would still be alive."

Tom hears this as he returns from outside to the dining room. Sandy thinks he looks a little shaky, or nervous.

"What is it, Tom?"

"It's too late to board up. The fog is on the road in front of the house. I can't even see the mailbox."

"What will we do?"

Tom clears his throat, "we will make sure all windows and doors are locked. We will continue to try reaching 911. Maybe the phones will work. Then we will stay here in the dining room. If anyone breaks in, we will get to the basement as fast as possible and try to hole up until we can get some help. Bobby, I don't want you to be scared, these are all just precautions."

Bobby looks at his father and says, "the scary man is ugly, and I don't like him. But I could hear him talking to me in my mind. I didn't hear him with my ears, I heard him with my mind. I don't think we need to worry about him. We need to worry about each other."

"We love each other, we are a family. Why would you say that?" Sandy doesn't like that Bobby would say such a thing.

"Because the scary man can get in your head. He can't get in our house unless we let him in, but he can get inside your head. And when he was in my head, a part of me wanted to open the door for him. I know what it feels like to have him inside your head and he does and says terrible things. I ran from him because I feared him. But mostly, I ran from him because I was scared of me."

126

Within the Fog

20

Mearl stares through the door peephole. Sin stands near him, peeking through the curtains at the side of the living room window. They have been standing here long enough that Sin feels his back cramp. He knows better than to leave his watch. His dad seems intent on delivering his brand of justice to whoever has been ringing their doorbell. Crouching at the window, he tries to forget about his pain.

Finally, Mearl has also had enough. "Alright, them little Wells fags has smartened up and gone home to their cryin' papa. Let's go back and eat." Mearl has had a long-standing feud with Mr. Wells. Sin hopes it wasn't the two teenage Wells boys pranking them because that will just incite Mearl to start a conflict with the Wells family all over again. It is embarrassing to Sin because he goes to school with both Wells sons.

Following his father to the table, he hopes that is the end of the doorbell ringing. He also hopes Mearl gets drunk enough tonight to pass out earlier than usual. And he hopes he gets drunk enough that he forgets about his invitation to Rita for a barbeque. As he plops down to a now cold bowl of chili the doorbell rings. He looks at his father and thinks, oh shit, here we go.

"Those rotten little sons of bitches, I ain't puttin up with their shit, not another damned minute!" Mearl pushes his bowl of chili across the table and staggers into the dining room wall. Regaining his balance, he stomps to the living room. Sin hustles to catch up to his father and looks out the curtains at the window at the same time Mearl looks through the peephole.

"Hot Damn, I knew it! And them boys have grown some full-sized man balls, standin' there on my damn stoop. Alright, are you ready, Sin? You and me is family, and family sticks together. Them boys is almost grown men, so you need to have your old man's back." Mearl absent mindedly scratches at his right temple.

"Dad wait just a second. I don't see anyone on the stoop. There's no one there." Sin hopes he doesn't get hit in his head for telling Mearl, but he is puzzled and wonders how many beers his father drank tonight.

"What the hell are you goin' on about? Them boys is standin' there on the stoop. Let's just open up and see what they want." Mearl gives Sin a murderous stare. "You ain't pussin out on me, is you?"

"No dad, I'm not, but I'm looking out there and all I see is the fog. I don't see either of the Wells kids. I don't see anybody at all. I swear."

"Oh bullshit, hush up your lyin' mouth, and let's go see why them fags keeps ringing the dang doorbell." Mearl continues massaging the side of his head.

At that exact moment, almost as though Mearl has wished it to happen with his words, the doorbell rings again. Mearl sighs, "Ya see? Now move over."

Sin looks out the curtain, and again there is no one outside that he can see. "Dad, something is wrong here. There's no way they could have run fast enough for me to not see them ringing the bell."

"Dammit, they didn't run nowhere. Theys standin' right. Out. There." Mearl stresses his frustration with exaggerated pointing at the front door. "If you ain't gonna help, move out of my way."

Sin steps aside but has a strange feeling that something is wrong. There is something wrong with the fog, and he feels as though the situation is about to get much worse. Mearl unlocks the deadbolt and throws open the door.

"Well, hello there my good neighbors from up the road. Before either of you runs your yaps, can you tell me exactly why it is you need to ring my bell a hunerd times tonight?" Mearl looks very satisfied with himself. It is his 'I caught you red-handed' look, but Sin only slightly registers this. More than what Mearl is saying, Sin focuses on the empty front porch stoop.

Sin thinks, Dad must have started drinking far earlier than I thought because he is talking to an empty front stoop. How in the world am I going to get him to stop this tonight?

"Oh is that right, huh? Ain't you gonna defend yourself, boy?" Mearl is staring at Sin. The 'I caught you red-handed' look is now focused on Sin.

"What do you mean?"

"Are you deaf? Young Mr. Wells here says that Rita is a made-up name. There is no Rita. Is this so? And don't you lie to your old man."

"Dad, Rita is my friend. I go to school with her and she is real. Why do you think that?"

"You is lyin boy. And ah–ha!," Mearl slaps his head in recognition of something astounding that has occurred to him, "That's why we haven't had the honor of miss Rita's presence for dinner. She ain't real."

Mearl grabs Sin by his neck. "Sorry to have to embarrass you in front of these here Wells boys but at least theys good enough to tell me the truth about you. My own damn son." Mearl shakes his head in disgust and throws Sin out of the house onto the stoop. "After this here night, you won't even think about lyin' to me again." Sin slides back on his rear end until he is partially falling off the stoop.

"Dad, listen, something is wrong with you. It's just you and me here. There is no one else. Look around, we are alone."

Mearl sighs and shakes his head again as he rolls up his sleeves. He steps out of the house, looks into the empty fog and says, "I'm sure sorry you boys have to see this, but I do preciate you stoppin' by and tellin' me the truth."

As Mearl bends to grab at Sin, a shadow from above them both blots out the little daylight that remains. Sin looks up in time to see something that immediately has him questioning his eyesight. The dark figure of a man, a man with wings coming

132

out of his back, descends on his father. Mearl notices Sin looking beyond him and turns to follow his son's gaze. The man from above slashes out a hand that has incredibly long, yellowed nails and snatches up Mearl by his neck. A startled yelp escapes Mearl as his neck bends at an impossible angle. That is the last Sin sees of Mearl as the winged man shoots straight up into the fog at an incredible rate of speed. Both the winged man and his father are gone. Sin stares up for a further glimpse of either of them, but only sees the disturbed mists of the fog settle back into place. He knows that he needs to get back inside his house and that knowledge is punctuated by more shadows from above. Determining that there are more of the winged men in the fog above him, Sin throws himself into his home slamming the door shut on the insanity of the last few minutes.

21

"Alright, we have the supplies we need in the basement. We have enough food for several days." Tom says to Sandra and Bobby, "and we are now completely surrounded by fog." He looks to the windows in the kitchen, sees the gray mist of the fog, and pulls the curtain closed on the window. "We know what we know, which gives us a little information to think through. Hopefully, nothing comes of this other than a fog bank that clears up by morning." As Tom says this, he doesn't believe it will go that way, but hope springs eternal. "Oh, and I tried dialing 911 from both of our phones, but they're still not working. We can keep trying, of course."

Sandy smiles and recognizes that for now, they have done all they can. They need to sit down now and get as much information together as they can so they can to best determine how to deal with whatever is going on in the fog. She, like Tom, is praying that nothing will come of this, but they need to figure out a strategy, if possible.

"All right guys, let's heat up some leftovers from the fridge and eat. Then we will talk."

The Benton's put their arms around each other, Bobby sandwiched in the middle, and make their way to the refrigerator unaware that they will not have to wait long to have that small bit of hope for an uneventful night smashed into a billion pieces.

THE BEGINNING OF THE END

Fear. Anger. Sadness. These emotions created the most delicious consumption of the human being. Human meat and blood were their only sustenance. When fueled by powerful emotions like fear, anger, and sadness the taste of a human became electric on the tongue and created an almost dizzying effect on the mind. Blood, bone, meat, and tendon. All satisfied the deep burning inside of them. They could, and sometimes did, eat animals, but the human body was the only solution to their hunger. It was a long-awaited taste and experience, for many years could pass before the next feeding.

In his previous life as a human, he had vague memories of these emotions, but the virus he acquired in Europe in the late 1400s had removed his humanity. He felt no sorrow or empathy for those he consumed. Humanity was food with a few rules. The virus was a curse, or the curse was the virus, but something had always prevented his kind from annihilating humanity. The inability to gain immediate access to where they hid from him kept it so. It was impossible to gain entry to a human's home without a human opening a door or window. Humans had to create that entry. The myth that his kind needed an invitation was incorrect. He needed no invitation, just an opening that he could not create. Humans didn't have to invite him in, but they had to make access available. As frustrating as this could be when the hunger was raging inside of him, he always got the most stubborn of the little pigs.

His vision had changed with the virus. He couldn't see humans as he had before. After he had been infected, he started seeing them as intense, red, glowing beings like fire in the shape of a human. He could detect their energy and see the blood flow within them. Seeing that blood could drive him and his kind into a frenzy like that of piranha feeding on a dying animal carcass. He had supernatural strength, even beyond others of his kind. He could see a human through walls and hear their speech in the same manner. He could fly when his strength was at its peak. He could sense human emotions and he could manipulate those emotions, although he had to be near to get within their minds. The game was always simple. If humans were outside, he would terrorize them until he could smell the fear reeking out of their pores. They tasted better when they were terrorized. If a human was inside a dwelling or structure, the challenge was to get within their minds, their consciousness. He would manipulate them until they opened a door or window or came outside. Either way, the result was the same, he would feed.

It was about his kind's existence, and the pleasure the game and the feeding created. Humans didn't stand a chance against them because humans were weak. They lacked morality, and they created the misery in their own lives. He and his kind used humanity's immorality to manipulate the strong emotions needed. They needed to feed within four days of beginning the hunt. He couldn't sustain the required energy to hunt and feed for longer than four days and still survive in his resting state. If he hunted beyond four days, he began aging and it was not reversible. He had learned this the hard way over the centuries.

Human men and women had always been so concerned with ruling the earth that his kind had been reduced to fictional characters. A blind man did not see danger coming, and humanity had become blinded by arrogance. Mankind had labeled himself the master of the earth and in so doing had become the blind. Humans were easy targets, and when it was time to feed, the game began. He led his kind to small towns. Places that were remote and isolated. If humanity ever discovered their existence, they could be destroyed. So, he chose small towns where there were enough humans to satisfy the deep, burning hunger that had driven them for centuries. They never left behind any trace of killing or evidence of the slaughter. There was no reason to encourage humanity to question if it was remotely possible that he and his kind existed.

Each time a town had been discovered with meals sitting on tables uneaten, not a human within sight, mankind shrugged their collective shoulders and went back to their corrupt lives of egotism and materialistic satisfaction. When his victims attempted to leave behind clues about his existence, humanity was never willing to look closely enough to figure out the truth. He had been alive and well for centuries. He remembered each hunt. Places that had died overnight at his hands. He savored watching the pigs quivering and shaking in fear, desperately throwing open doors to escape horrific mirages. He created these visions from their memories and emotions. He could see fragments of memories and he could feel their emotions. When feeding he could taste their fear. They opened doors to him because of visions that did not exist. They ran through streets screaming in fear as he tore them limb from limb, catching droplets of blood on his tongue as it rained from the sky.

He only hated about himself that he had been born from humanity. He needed humans, craved them, but they repulsed him with their weakness. They were pigs. His kind, his clan, was comprised of those who were more like the old guard of humanity. Those who were strong, and those who were angry. Mankind had drifted far from the men and women who had settled new wild territories and explored hostile lands. They had been tough. When he came across a human with these qualities, a human brimming with anger and hostility, someone who hated his fellow man, he offered to turn them. He gave them eternal life on earth. These humans were rare, only encountering one or two each century, and most of them accepted his offer, his call to dominion over mankind. Today most of humanity was like cattle being raised and fattened up for the feast. And feast he had through the years. He feasted at Easter Island in 1718. He feasted at Hoer Verde, Brazil, in 1923. He feasted at Lake Anjikuni, Nunavut, Canada in 1930. And he feasted at Roanoke, Virginia in 1590 along with many other places around the world.

Roanoke, where Becca had refused his offer of eternal life. She had been tough but lacked the hate, the internal anger that had driven so many to him. Mankind was his sustenance, and it was he

140

who was the master of all he surveyed. He was Croatoan.

Croatoan turns his attention to the house before him. Within he can see three burning human shapes. The boy he has been visiting at night, the woman who he almost had in his grasp in the small town earlier that evening, and a man who he had not had the pleasure of visiting. The time had arrived. The three before him represented the end of this feast. This last game tonight would be the best. His hunger had been satisfied earlier in the night. These three represented one last game. He looks to the remaining four of his kind who had yet to feast and smiles with rows of jagged teeth protruding from his blood-soaked mouth. Three females and another male. All others in his clan had feasted on this night and so he had sent them back to their nest to sleep.

One female holds a limp Sabrina Sellers close to her. The names of these four do not matter to him as he can feel their essence and the satisfaction they will feel from feeding. The boy will be a tasty little pig. The woman will be a challenge, but he knows he can break her. There is something inside her that still struggles, and he will find its source. The man? Who knows? It will be a pleasure to find out, and he hopes the man is strong. There is still

141

plenty of time on this night of hunting to play with his prey. He has until dawn and then his time for this hunt will be done. Plenty of time remains. He will feel the man slowly descend into madness and before he is done, the man, woman and child will beg for release. He will chew and tear, and he will feel their bones snap within his bite, and he will pulverize and drink and swallow until there are only red stains seeping into the ground to prove these pigs had ever existed. Once accomplished, he will return to his home and he will sleep. The sleep of the dead.

Without speaking a word, he communicates his instructions to the other four and descends upon the isolated house within the fog. The fog that has always protected his private hunting grounds.

CONFRONTATION

1

The three of them sit at the table, having satisfied their hunger with leftover barbequed ribs, coleslaw, green beans, and buttered rolls. It was a dinner fit for three people living in the country. Tom only lamented they could not eat on the back patio that was so often a part of their summer landscape. The backyard is surrounded by golden pastures that sway in summer breezes, the garage, and large rows of shrubs that give a sense of boundary to the private patio area. As they sit in the dining room staring at the dirty dishes, Sandy sighs and leans forward, elbows on the table, sagging under the weight of a healthy dinner and the weight of their circumstances. She feels tired and going to bed and sleeping until the fog is gone is very appealing. Based on their discussion, however, that won't happen.

"Well, we don't know much, do we?"

Tom looks at his wife and can't shake the feeling that she is not well, but he acknowledges that

143

she has had some extreme shocks today. It surprises him she ate as well as she had during dinner. "Although we don't know everything and can't explain even part of what has happened, we know a bit." Sandy and Bobby stare at him, waiting for his explanation. "For instance, let's assume that it is this man who came to Bobby's window, and he murdered Ruth. As crazy as that sounds, we know that he could not follow Bobby when he ran from the room. Also, remember what I heard the man on the ham radio say. He said that they can't come in unless you allow them. He specifically said 'they'. If he was talking about this same man who was at Bobby's window, it backs up what Bobby feels, which is that this man needs us to let him in. He can't come in on his own. It would also indicate that he is not alone." Sandy looks at him as though he is taking an extreme leap in concluding these things.

"Tom, we don't even know that Bobby didn't have a night terror and dream the man."

"Mom, I didn't dream of him. He's real." Bobby's frustration shows in his tone.

"I know you're convinced Bobby, and I'm sorry, I don't want you to think I don't believe you. It's just that this is so outside of the box, I still can't even believe what I saw in town. I guess I need to

144

prepare as though all this is real and change my thinking. It's hard to take. Something that strong and capable of taking a human being into the air and dropping them..." Sandy shakes her head as if in denial.

"Listen, honey, let's prepare for the worst." As Tom says this Bobby gets up from the table and heads into the living room. "And if we are wrong about this, we will keep the secret of our craziness to ourselves, so no one has us committed." Tom's attempt at lightening the mood is an obvious failure as neither his wife nor his son reacts to him.

"Bobby, don't be mad at mommy okay? I've just had a bad day. A terrible day." There is no answer from Bobby in the living room.

"Give him a moment, he needs to come to terms with all of this." Tom stops her from getting up from the table and holds her hand. "We know that for some reason this man was not seeing Bobby through his window. Or at least that's what it seems like. There seems to be more than one of whatever that man is, and Bobby is convinced they're in the fog. It's like the fog is home for this man, or them if that's the case. We better hope that they can't just break a window and come in because that is where we are most vulnerable."

Sandy looks at Tom but is not focused on him, or even his actual words. She understands the meaning of what he's saying, but she is much more focused on how helpless she feels. She wishes she had Tom's resilience.

"Tom, what will we do if they try to get in?"

"We head straight to the basement. Lock ourselves in and prepare to shoot anything that comes down the stairs."

2

Croatoan watches the house from the cocoon of fog within the shadows of the front yard. He can see the three burning human shapes sitting together inside the house. He can hear bits and pieces of their conversation. The three humans are trying to reason out a plan for dealing with him. It seems like they expect him to show up here, as he has. That's good, he thinks, it would be nice for this game to present a challenge. He cannot hear everything said, but he doubts they know or understand anything of value. That's unlikely. He waits for his opening, and finally gets it as the smallest of the three red, pulsing human shapes walks through the house in his direction.

Croatoan steps out from behind shrubs and onto the front porch, on the other side of the wall where the boy named Bobby sits down. He can feel the boy's energy and it is that of anger. So much the better. Croatoan reaches out through the distance between himself and the boy on the other side of the wall. It can take a great deal of energy to trespass inside the mind of a human, but it is worth it once the feeding begins. He feels the boy, and he pushes a little harder to penetrate the invisible shield of the boy's mind. The key to this has always been to get the human to feel as though he is creating the thoughts places in their heads. He reaches into Bobby's mind and he can see images of the boy's parents and feel the anger the boy has for them. This is good, he thinks, very good.

3

Bobby sits sulking in the living room. When will his parents treat him like he's not a baby? He has told them a million times about the man at his window. He was there. And still they act like he was having a nightmare. The man will end up eating us because they refuse to believe me, he says to himself. What he ought to do is teach them a lesson. He knows that if he goes outside, the man will come to him. If he did that he could run back inside and shut the door and then call his parents to the living room. They would look out the windows and see the man, and then they would know that he is real. That would teach his parents. He could see his mom in his mind, crying and apologizing for not believing him. And that would serve her right. It was about time they started respecting him as a young man. He was almost nine years old and no longer in diapers. He is old enough to do dishes and have chores, so he is also old enough to know the difference between a bad dream and reality. All he'd have to do is go to the door, open it up and take one step outside. One little step and the man would come to him. Then his mom would see he wasn't some crybaby loser who needed to make up stories to get attention.

149

Bobby scratches the right side of his head. He feels like an itch has burrowed deeply into his brain, and then it is gone and far from his thoughts.

One step out, that's all that's needed. One step out and the man can come. He can drift through the fog and show his mom he's real. Show both of his parents, and he will show them. This feels right, it's a good plan. I'm glad I left the dining room and came in here. Now that I'm not listening to my parents, I can come up with good ideas of my own. And this is a great idea. I just need to get up and walk to the door. Bobby feels relief. He will soon be as respected as he wishes to be, and then he can tell both of his parents he is right, and they are wrong.

Bobby gets off the couch and starts walking toward the front door.

4

"Tom, if that man is real, and there is more than him... If they come here to get inside but can't break-in, how will they get inside?"

"Well, Bobby heard the man in his mind, which makes sense because it isn't likely he heard him through a closed window. He was trying to get Bobby to let him inside, so the man could," Tom clears his throat a little, "so the man could eat us. So, I'm guessing somehow he needs us to let him inside."

"We would never do that, so if that's all there is to this we can just sit inside and wait until they're gone. That shouldn't be a problem."

"Well yeah, but..."

"What?" Sandy wants this all to go away, so she doesn't want Tom to ruin her theory.

"Sands, listen to me. I don't know what this man is, but if he can float outside our son's second-story window and speak inside our minds, he might very well be able to trick us into letting him in. He may mess with our minds and manipulate us. I don't want to believe that's possible, but we need to think about that or at least be aware."

Sandy feels like she has forgotten something, and then she realizes why. "Speaking of our son, he's awfully quiet. What's he doing?"

Both look to the living room and call their son "Bobby!"

5

Bobby has arrived at the front door and stands staring at it for a moment in confusion. I was sitting on the couch, and now I am here. How did I get here? And then he feels a renewed sense of anger and it comes back to him. I'm here because I'm going to let Croatoan inside our house. He will come inside, and he will eat us all like the little pigs we are. This random thought scares him and he thinks of course he wouldn't ever do that. I'm not sure why I would even think something like that. I don't feel like me, but I am me. Wait, what was it I was thinking about? I can't remember, but I know that I have a good plan. Oh, that's right, I plan to go outside. But why am I going outside?

I had a good idea to go outside and ......

He reaches for the handle on the front door. It feels cold in his hands. More like it would feel in winter, not in July.

My idea....my idea was to scare some sense into my damn mom. She never believes me. Well, I'll show her, I'll show her and my dad. I'll call that scary man right to us and then I'll shut the door and

then they'll see I'm not lying. They will see that...
I... am.... NOT..... A.... BABY! They'll learn a
lesson. I'll show them they're the dirty pigs that I
know they are. I'll show them..... they're food.
They're meat bags. The little pigs are scared, and all
I need to do is open the door.

Bobby turns the door handle.

6

"Tom, he's not answering us. Let's go see what's going on."

As they stand from the table Tom tells Sandy, "I'm sure he's fine, he's just mad at us because we are pigs and we are scared."

Sandy stops walking, "What did you say?" She watches Tom as he scratches the side of his head.

Tom looks at his wife with a blank expression, "I said he is scared. That's all, he'll be fine."

Sandy shakes her head; I must be more tired than I even realized she thinks. The two of them walk again to the living room.

7

Croatoan has moved step for step with the burning form of the boy on the other side of the wall, to the front door. The boy hesitates as he places his hand on the door handle. He reaches further into the boy's mind with his anger, feeling that the boy is close to giving him what he wants. Just a little further…. The door handle turns.

8

Tom enters the living room ahead of his wife. When he sees Bobby turning the front door handle it is as if time is moving in slow motion. The handle turns in Bobby's hand. Another quarter turn and the door will spring open. It never occurs to him that Bobby or any of them would even think about opening the door to the monster outside. He yells Bobby's name and in the same instant he feels Sandy as she tries to push past him to get to their son. Bobby does not react to hearing his name and continues to turn the handle. Tom is close enough now that he can see Bobby's face from the side. He notices a small silver drop of drool hanging from Bobby's chin. Bobby looks distant and vacant. Little wisps of fog begin to flow in the open crack of the door. A part of his brain marvels at the strange things that stand out in a moment of crisis.

"Bobby, NO!" Sandy yells at their son and launches herself in front of Tom like a missile. Sandy slams into the door and it bangs shut. Tom reaches the door and pushes the lock back in place. He and Sandy look at each other in recognition of their near disaster.

"Bobby, what in God's name are you doing?" Sandy is yelling as she tries to stand and face her son.

"Sands, look at him." Tom grabs Bobby by the shoulders and turns him to face his mother. Sandy gasps and her tone shifts from one of great anger to one of great worry.

"Bobby? Look at me. Tom, what's wrong with him?"

Bobby mumbles something incoherent under his breath and continues to stare slack-jawed into an unseen abyss. Tom picks him up and retreats to the dining room, with Sandy on his heels.

9

Croatoan has complete control of Bobby, and it is draining him. The little pig is strong, and hard to keep under his direction. Bobby has more anger in him than he expected. He is about to relinquish control of the boy as the door handle turns as far as it can and the door pops open. As his jaw opens and his enormous teeth protrude, the door slams shut. He has been so consumed with controlling the little pig that he didn't see the bigger pigs coming to the rescue. The three family members burn a deep red on the other side of the door. The hue of red burns bright with their fear and he can almost taste it on his black tongue. The blood flows in their bodies and he watches it circulate through them, pulsing with the beats of their hearts. His right hand reaches out to them. If he could, he would launch himself through the door and tear them apart. But he cannot, as he never has been able. The door was open and now it is closed.

I can feel their heat and smell their fear, but I cannot yet taste their blood, their meat.

A deep growl escapes his throat, and he retreats from the front porch. He will need to recover his strength and find another way. The little pig is too far from him now as the family has gone back to the center of the house, and he is far too tired.

Yes, run pigs, run away, but I am here, and you will be mine!

He pushes this thought at the three of them as hard as he can in a sudden burst of anger. It hits their minds, and he laughs when he feels all three of them jerk in sudden fear.

He remembers the old lady. Lovely Sabrina Sellers. He hoped that he wouldn't need to use her because it meant exposing himself, but this is a game and he will win it as he always does. His laughter grows, and he is most pleased with himself for his restraint. He had wanted to kill Sabrina the moment she had come out of her house. She is weak and pathetic. But he had resisted that temptation and it would now pay off.

I'll be back shortly Benton clan, and I always keep my promises. Don't I Sabrina?

He can feel the woman squirm at the mention of her name as she waits in the arms of the female that hold her.

Within the Fog

10

"Tom, was that him? Did you hear that voice? He is out there, and he wants to kill us," The sympathy Sandy feel for Bobby has grown exponentially now that she has heard the man speak into her mind. The nights he had run to her and Tom's room in terror put a weight on her heart. She had failed him. The three of them arrive back in the dining room and sit at the table. Bobby is so far unresponsive to them and Tom has placed him on Sandy's lap.

Tom replies, "Yes. That was him."

"He's here. And he was in Bobby's head. That's why Bobby was opening the door. It was him. And you and I heard the same thing, and we heard that in our minds too." Sandy is shocked and for the first time, she understands how bleak their situation has become.

"Sandy, remember that Bobby said the man didn't see him when he ran from his room?"

"Yes, we discussed that, why?"

"Because just now he saw us moving from the living room door back here to the dining room. He said we were running away."

"Yes, I heard that too." Sandy is trying to process the meaning of this information.

"Why couldn't he see Bobby, but he definitely could see us." Tom is lost under his furrowed brow, "there's something to that we need to figure out."

"I hate this."

"I do too, but we have to think. Our lives are in substantial danger. I guess we can't call him a man anymore, but whatever he is, we need to figure him out. We know that he can't let himself inside which is good, and we also know that he can crawl inside our heads which is very bad. This is all real Sandy. We will not be able to be out of each other's sights. Especially Bobby." Tom looks at his son and grabs his shoulders, "Come on Bobby, wake up."

Tom shakes Bobby as he sits slack against Sandy.

Bobby blinks his eyes and seems to finally have gained some clarity regarding where he is and what has happened, "I didn't know it was him. I swear. I kept thinking I wanted to go outside, but it wasn't me thinking that, it was him. It was the scary man. He got inside of me and I was convinced I needed to go outside." Bobby is back with them and while they are both relieved to have him back, Tom can't help but wonder why Bobby thought he needed to go outside. While Sandy holds Bobby on her lap hugging him to her chest, Tom gently asks Bobby what happened.

"Bobby, what did he make you think to convince you to open the door?"

"I remember being mad at you guys because you weren't listening to me. He could sense that because he used my anger against me. I thought I was doing the right thing trying to open the door." Bobby pauses and then continues, "I wanted to show you guys you were wrong to not believe me and he used that. And he's strong, but his control of me was getting weaker the longer he was in my head. I could feel that I wanted to open the door, but it felt like I was struggling to remember why I wanted to open it. It didn't make sense."

"Bobby, I'm just glad you are back with us, you had us scared for a minute." Tom ruffles Bobby's hair and Bobby smiles at his dad.

"I'm sorry I got mad at you guys."

Sandy brushes aside a tear that has escaped its jail and runs down her cheek, "It's me that owes you an apology Bobby, I'm sorry for not believing you. Forgive me?"

"Of course mom." Sandy hugs him tighter and he laughs and then starts squirming in her grasp. She kisses his cheeks in response, and he squeals and tries to escape her, "Ah, c'mon mom, I'm not that little anymore."

"You might be growing up mister, but you'll never be too old for kisses from your mom." She pokes him in his tummy, and he laughs.

"Not even when I'm thirty years old?"

"Nope, not even then."

11

Croatoan stands motionless, surrounded by his fog. The mist wraps around him and provides comfort and strength. He is recharging. He can hear the laughter inside the house. They are too far away to know what is making them laugh, but he cannot stand the sound of them. Laughter is a bitter taste. Fear creates the succulent taste he craves. He wants to split the father in half and feed him to the woman and child before he and his kind consume them. The pigs are laughing, and it enrages him and fills him with the energy he needs to finish this game. You won't be laughing for long, he thinks, soon you'll be crying and begging for your lives. And my promise to you is that I will deny you escape. You will feed the remaining of my kind who haven't feasted this night, and I will make sure I get to feed again. Maybe I will eat the little pig, maybe I will eat one of the older pigs, but I will eat. He reaches out in silent communication across the yard to the male who awaits instructions and he sends them. A minute later, the lights in the Benton house blink out.

12

Sandy sits in the dining room, watching Tom mentally process everything they have experienced and all that they know. She has been so worried over protecting Bobby and coming to terms with this crisis that she had completely forgotten that she had left her Xanax in the car. She had parked the car in the detached garage. This is an issue, and it is an issue of significance because she has now not taken her pills for three days. To worsen this issue, she has lied to Tom about it. They are surrounded by a deep fog; with something they couldn't define that wanted them dead. The path to her medication went straight through that enemy. She didn't know how she could get her pills. She didn't know if she could figure out a way to get them on her own, but she doubted it. After what they had been through, with Bobby almost letting in the very evil they were trying to keep away, she didn't think she should chance doing something that had the potential of being idiotic. This led her to the conclusion that she was going to have to tell Tom. She could feel the need for her medication growing as she slipped into the dark corners of depression.

"Tom, I need to ......"

Sandy is cut off as the lights go out and the hum of the refrigerator winds to a stop. The house becomes silent.

"It's him, isn't it?" Sandy has forgotten all about her medication and looks at the nearest windows, expecting one of them to shatter.

"Yes, I believe it is."

"Why did he cut our power?"

"Intimidation, he's planning something, I'm not sure."

From outside their home, in the front yard, they hear whimpers, followed by a shrill cry.

"What is that, Tom?"

"The better question is – Who is that? Let's go have a look." Tom rises from his chair at the dining room table.

"Tom is that wise? Maybe we should just stay here."

"How about you two stay here and I'll go have a quick peek? I know we shouldn't be apart, so

I'll take a quick peek and come right back. We need to be aware of what's going on out there."

Sandy nods her agreement but adds, "Be quick, okay?"

"I will, I'll be fast."

Tom tiptoes through the house and realizes that he's trying to be quiet and has no idea why. He slides up to the front window and peeks through the curtains. He can't hide the shock at what he sees.

"Oh, shit." The words escape his mouth before he can reel them back in, and in no time Sandy and Bobby are at his side.

"What's wrong?"

"Hon, I think you should wait in the dining room and I'll be back in a moment."

Sandy is as nervous as Tom has ever seen her and she wants nothing to do with his idea, "No, we all stick together. What's wrong?"

Tom moves to the front door peephole and Sandy steps into his place at the window. As soon as he peers outside, the three of them hear the voice of their enemy.

169

Well, hello, Tom. There you are. Where is the rest of your clan?

Tom says to Sandy, "He knows my name. How does he know my name?"

How do I know all that I know? Well, Tom, I suggest you come outside, and I can explain it to you. In fact, it would help your neighbor here tremendously.

Sandy mouths the words to Tom, "He can hear us. He's hearing what you are saying. Is that Sabrina?"

Tom makes eye contact with Bobby and points to the note tablet and pen sitting on the coffee table behind him. Bobby grabs it and hands it to his father. Quickly Tom scribbles a message to Sandy and holds it up.

It's Sabrina. He hears us, but he can't see you. He only sees me.

Understanding washes over Sandy's face and she takes the tablet from Tom and writes a new note under his:

We're in front of the window. He was outside of Bobby's window. He can't see through the glass. It's the glass. Has to be.

Sandy hands Tom the notepad, and after he reads it, she points to the window for emphasis.

Tom? Your friend here would like to see you. Open the door and come on out.

From outside comes another shriek. Tom peeks back out at Sabrina standing in the clutches of a female figure clad in black. She looks exhausted and lifeless. So, there is more than him, Tom thinks. He can see the man that Bobby described to him on the other side of Sabrina, and he has Sabrina's arm in his grasp. Tom realizes that he can see the three figures in his front yard because the fog has cleared between them and his front door. The fog is everywhere else, but a convenient path has opened in a direct line from his door, from him to them. They are too far away to see clearly, but he does not doubt this being the man Bobby described. Feeling overwhelmed, he wants to help Sabrina but isn't sure how.

"Listen, you don't need to hurt her. Let her come to us and I'll open the door and let her inside. She looks injured, she needs help." Tom looks to

Sandy and shrugs, communicating to her he doesn't know what to do or say.

That's a very kind offer, but I will politely decline Thomas. I prefer the formality of given names; you don't mind if I call you Thomas?

"I prefer Tom. Let Sabrina come inside."

You do realize you are in no position to make demands, Thomas.

Tom knows he has no power in this conversation and becomes even more concerned about Sabrina. He runs through scenario after scenario trying to figure out a way to help her and comes up only with doing as the man wishes. But to do that would mean jeopardizing the safety of Sandy and Bobby. He feels sick as his stomach churns.

"I'm also in no position to *do* as you say, and you know this. What do you want?"

Sandy is peering through the window and Bobby keeps trying to get next to her to see outside. She keeps moving him back and finally, Tom reaches over and grabs Bobby by the arm and gives him a look of disapproval that only a dad can give. Bobby stops what he is doing and for the smallest of seconds anger flashes across Bobby's features and then it is gone.

The only position you have IS to do as I say. I want you to come outside. Come outside or Sabrina will suffer.

I need to buy some time, Tom thinks and says, "I am at a disadvantage. You know who I am, but I don't know you. What is your name?"

As it was written at Roanoke, it is today. Come out now Thomas, we have much to discuss and your friend Sabrina would very much like to see you.

Sandy grabs the pad and pen back from Tom and writes her question.

Written at Roanoke?

Tom takes the note pad back from Sandy, and under her question provides her with the answer.

Croatoan. It's what was written at Roanoke, Virginia when that colony disappeared. Late 1500s.

Upon reading the name, Sandy remembers they watched a History Channel show on the lost colony of Roanoke, Virginia. There had been over a hundred people who had disappeared and had never been found. If the man outside was responsible for that, he had completely decimated the colony. She also realizes that if what he says about Roanoke is true, it makes him impossibly old and incredibly powerful.

"Roanoke, that was a long time ago. That would make you several hundred years old. Croatoan."

Time flows like a river in many directions. Age is a perception based on the only frame of reference you have. Speaking of time, Thomas, you have had more than enough. Come out.

Tom is running out of ideas and he won't be able to stall the man outside for much longer and so he takes a risk.

"My son says you wanted him to let you into our home so you could eat us."

Such active imaginations children have. Of course, my appearance can cause quite a fright, especially in the young. Come out now Thomas, I grow weary of this.

"You know I can't do that. You told Bobby you were hungry, and you were going to eat us."

Tom can see a fine film of sweat has broken out across his wife's forehead. She is scared and now hugging Bobby to her from behind. He feels terrible guilt in not going outside to help Sabrina, and yet he can't risk the lives of his family. Tom jumps back at the sound of a thump against the front door. He recovers and again peers through the peephole. The man, Croatoan, is on the other side and he is glaring at the lens Tom sees through. For the first time, Tom realizes there are no whites to his eyes. His eyes are entirely black. His skin is white and almost casting light, like the glow sticks Bobby had last year on Halloween.

Croatoan has Sabrina laying on her side, holding her by her hair as if she is a dead rabbit he has hunted and brought home. She is not a person; she is his possession. He raises the arm that clutches Sabrina and she screams in pain. Stumbling, she attempts to get to her feet.

"Don't hurt her!" Tom yells as he watches Sabrina's face contort in pain.

Then come outside PIG.

175

Tom locks eyes with Sabrina as she glances at the door, "Sabrina, I'm so sorry."

"Don't open Tom, Steve is dead. And so am I." Sabrina says the words and makes no further attempts to speak as she stumbles back to her knees.

Croatoan remains expressionless.

As it is said, so it is done.

Croatoan's arm moves faster than Tom's mind can comprehend, and Sabrina goes from his front porch to landing in his yard, airborne for what seems an eternity. When she lands, her leg snaps and her foot bends at an unnatural angle. She cries out in anguish and twists on the ground in pain for only a moment when four dark blurs descend on her. Tom's brain lags his vision, and then he realizes that he is seeing the shape of four people tearing Sabrina into shreds of skin and muscle with their mouths. Blood and tissue fly in every direction and Tom slides down the inside of his front door into a heap on the floor.

"Take Bobby to the dining room."

Sandy, pale even in the shadows of the dark living room, doesn't question him as she knows that what happened outside is the end of their friend.

"He killed her, didn't he?" Bobby asks looking from of his parents to the other. Tom can only nod his head once.

"Come on Bobby, let's go sit at the table, daddy will be right back."

Before this night is done Thomas, you will open that door and beg me to end you.

Tom rises to his feet. While turning his back to the front door and the monster on the other side he says, "I'll beg you for nothing you piece of shit.

177

13

"It's my fault she's dead, Sands."

"No, Tom, it isn't. There was nothing any of us could do. If you had gone out there, you would have been killed and," Sandy pauses and Bobby finishes her sentence for her, "eaten."

"She was our friend, and she needed us, Sandy, and we did nothing."

"She was our friend, but Tom, we did nothing because there was nothing we could do. And I'm afraid to say this out loud Tom, but I think we are dealing with…" She pauses, thinking for the millionth time how crazy she will sound, "they're vampires."

Tom has been holding his head in his hands and at this statement, he perks up in consideration of what Sandy has said. "Vampires," Tom repeats the word as he contemplates the man outside. "That makes sense if you think about it."

"I don't need to think about it for long Tom. They drink blood and eat flesh. And I don't want to keep thinking about it, I don't want to throw up." Sandy resists the impulse to gag.

"That's not all. If you think about how he couldn't see you and Bobby through the living room window, or Bobby through his bedroom window. It's almost like they use infrared to see. It's like the night vision goggles the military uses. They use heat signatures to turn the night into day, but those military goggles can't see heat through glass. That man, or vampire, Croatoan, whatever he is, didn't know you two were right beside me in the living room because you were behind glass. I think he sees our body heat."

"Don't forget that he could hear you speaking through the door. He could be listening to us even now."

"He may need to be closer to hear us. But to be sure maybe we need to ..." Tom stops speaking and with his right hand, gestures as though he is writing. "At least when it's important."

Tom leans toward his wife and son and lowers his voice to a whisper, "We will write to each other when it has to be secret. But if we stop talking altogether, he's going to get suspicious. Bobby, get in the cabinet behind us and grab some pens and a notebook for each of us."

179

Bobby grabs the items he is asked for and hands a pen and notebook to each of his parents. Immediately Sandy writes in her book.

It's the same thing for him to get inside of our minds. He has to be close to us. There seems to be a limit to his ability to maintain control. Bobby was out of his control after we brought him in here.

Tom reads Sandy's writing and responds on his notepad:

I agree, but we do not understand how much distance he needs to reach us. Maybe it depends on his strength, or maybe it's always the same for him. We just don't know. We have to be careful.

14

Croatoan stands over the remains of Sabrina. He signals for his clan to depart to the shadows of the yard. He will need to feed a little, for controlling the boy was far too draining of his strength. The need for additional sustenance is strong. Tonight was feeling like it may be more of a challenge than he thought. So be it. He had been through wars before and he had never lost. The losses he had experienced all had come as a human. He remembered his human wife of long ago. The cheating bitch. If he hadn't already murdered her while he was a human, he would have eaten her after the virus had turned him. With the virus raging through him, he would have relished her fear of him, and he would have savored every ounce of destroying her mind. And then he would have consumed her body piece by piece, keeping her alive to feel every bit of pain, for as long as he could. He kneels on the ground and eats while his mind rages over finding his wife in bed with a stranger those many hundreds of years before. Even then, before he became immortal, he reveled in stabbing her and her lover. He had watched the blood splash and flow across their bed of deceit and had felt the warmth of it bathe his skin. Eventually, the blood

181

had cooled, and with it her cries and begging for his forgiveness.

Forgiveness, what a ridiculous concept. Forgiveness was for the weak, for the pigs, and that slut had been a pig. The virus had infected him and blessed him with the strength to punish human weaknesses. He began destroying those who thought they gained some better place in life through simple-minded concepts such as forgiveness. He had none of the limitations of trepidation humans contemplated regarding life after death. No need to feel as though he needed to be a good person to gain life beyond his time on earth, for he would never need time beyond earth. The contemplations and contradictions of man had not been his for many years. The idiocy of mankind, living the lives of treachery they embraced only to get to the end of their lives, and in that moment of staring death in the face, seek forgiveness and redemption. Pathetic. They had no accountability for the havoc and the destruction they imposed on others. He destroyed humanity to feed and gain sustenance, but he found victory in ending the spread of their immoral corruption.

Before this night is over, he thinks, I will discover the weaknesses and corruption of the three pigs hiding inside their little home. I will exploit

182

those memories. I will seek their anger. I will use
those emotions to draw them out or to let me in,
and I will feed myself and the other four of my kind.
And then I will temporarily relinquish my anger and
settle for the embrace of sleep. And when I wake
and feel the hunger and rage renewed. I will find
another place. I will destroy and feed upon the weak
and the corrupt and again experience the electricity
as I taste their fear.

15

"Tom, listen, you're going to get angry with me so I'm apologizing in advance," Sandy whispers this across the dining room table and prepares for her husbands' reaction to what she has to say.

Tom's brow wrinkles at the mention of him potentially getting angry, "What's wrong?"

"Shhh! Tom, we have to whisper."

Tom lowers his voice. "Okay, I'm whispering."

"My happy pills are in the Outback. When I got home, I was in such a hurry to tell you about everything that I completely forgot the things I got at Sanders market, including my prescription."

Tom replies in a low voice, "Well, I'm not angry about that hon, I am concerned though that you won't have your medication. The worst-case scenario is that you may have to go without it today or a couple of days. You won't feel great, but I can't imagine this standoff going longer than that without help of some sort arriving."

"Unfortunately, that's not the worst case. The worst case is I am three days without the Xanax now and I'm not feeling well."

"Shit, Sands, I asked you if you were taking your meds. Why did you lie?" Tom's voice raises and Bobby is quick to put his fingers to his lips reminding him to be quiet. "Because of this! Because you get so angry. You make me not want to tell you anything when you get like this." Sandy can feel her emotions boiling, partially because she has not been taking the medication, although she won't admit that to Tom.

"I get angry, like anyone else, when I get lied to Sandy. It's not fair for you to blame me for being angry when you could have been honest when I asked you about the medication. Dammit." Tom tosses his notepad on the table and looks away, upset. "Okay, well here we are and now we have to get to the garage. You can't keep going without taking the pills, and you know it."

Sandy sits quietly. She doesn't respond to him because she knows he is right. She can't continue to go without the medication. She can feel the depression and the growing irritation she feels over things that shouldn't bother her at all. She can't help it even though she knows that what she feels is irrational. But she did screw up putting it off, and for that she is sorry.

"Tom, I am sorry. I'm sorry I put off going to the market for my refill. I'm sorry I lied to you and I'm sorry we have to get to the garage, but I'm starting to not feel well."

"Well, we don't have much of a choice," Tom remembers he had noticed she was off somehow. Now he knows why. "We have to get your pills and I have zero ideas on that. In case you didn't catch it, those things, those vampires, ate our friend out there. They jumped on her like a pack of wild dogs. They were fast Sandy. I've seen nothing like that. And the strength. He threw her backward from the porch with one arm and she landed twenty yards away. He tossed her like she weighed two pounds. And before she could even sit up these...." Tom is searching for the right word, "these blurs came out of the shadows and attacked. They ate her Sandy."

"Tom, stop. I can't hear any more of this."

"This is what we are up against and now we need to get your pills because you weren't taking them for the past three days." Tom looks beyond pissed, and even though she can't blame him, she's getting angry.

"I'll go get them. I'll figure it out. It's my
fault, so I'll be the one to get to the car." Sandy
places her hands in her lap to hide them from Tom.
Her hands are shaking because she is angry with
him. It was wrong for her to ignore picking up her
medication as she had, but he was wrong for treating
her like a child.

"No, you can't get angry and go out there.
We will have to create a distraction or something. If
you go out there without a plan, they'll do the same
thing they did to Sabrina. I need to spend a few
minutes thinking about this."

"I need to get up and move around a bit,
I've been sitting too much." Sandy gets up and
leaves the dining room.

Tom calls after her, "Don't be gone long.
We need to stay together."

Sandy wonders through the hallway and
then the living room. She paces back and forth by
the sofa. Like I need him to tell me that, she thinks.
He can be such a jerk. What would serve him right
is if I got up and went outside. I'd like to see the
look on his face. He'd learn to have a little sympathy
for me in this situation. She puts a shaking hand to
her temple and digs at the itch there.

Yeah, I screwed up, but at least I'm not a rude asshole. Sandy pauses and realizes that she is getting worked up, and it's not the right time for it. When this is all over, she will consider how to get Thomas, Tom to treat her better. Thomas? Where did that come from? She hadn't called him that in years other than when she was angry with him, which she certainly is now, so maybe that's why she thought of him as Thomas instead of Tom. None of that even matters, she reasons. What matters is that he is rude, he doesn't appreciate her, and he talks down to her. This caused so many issues in our marriage before she thinks. Once she began struggling with depression and anxiety, he had asserted himself. He had to be in control of everything. They were no longer a team. He was in charge just because she had some emotional issues. His dominance hadn't stopped even after the medication seemed to resolve those issues. It was still Thomas acting like her daddy. Like she needed someone to tell her what to do every second of the day. God, he could be so overbearing.

She could remember a time that he had decided he would take her medication and dole it out to her each day. She had asked him if he wanted a wife or another child. And he had responded that he didn't see her as a child, but he sure as hell had been treating her like one. She had thanked him kindly for his concern, but she would take her medication herself. He had gotten that whiny look on his face when she had said that to him and had replied with, "As long as you can remember, sometimes you get scattered." Well, if that hadn't just pissed her off. She had said nothing to him, because she didn't want to cause further problems, but she had wanted to smack him in his big, stupid, dumb Thomas face. Blah, blah, blah my name is Thomas and I'm smarter than everyone including my dimwitted wife Sandy.

Sandy paces back and forth in the living room, her hands trembling at her sides, tears rolling down her cheeks.

Well, fuck him, she thinks. I'll go get my damn pills. One time, years ago, they had been in the middle of an argument and she had threatened to leave. Thomas, the ever-brilliant master of all things Benton, had looked at her and said, "there's the door Sandy." Well, Sandy stops and looks at the front door. There it is. There is the front door and by God, if I want to use it, I will.

Sandy calls out to her husband, "Eat shit little Tommy do do! I'll do what I want."

As she attempts to step around the coffee table, she catches her toe on the edge of one table

189

leg. She promptly trips and lands with a thud after bouncing off the front of the sofa.

16

Tom is getting up to check on Sandy when he hears his wife's voice yelling to him.

"Eat shit little Tommy do do! I'll do what I want."

Bobby looks to his dad, "Huh?"

Tom pauses, thinking about the absurdity of what Sandy just yelled when they hear a crash and a groan. "Oh no, come on Bobby, we need to stay together!"

17

Croatoan had slipped inside of Sandy's mind the moment he sensed her nearing his position in the yard. She had anger. He couldn't see exactly why, but it was directed at her husband and he began using this as soon as he could feel it. Yes, Sandy, be angry. Tom speaks down to you and that impulse you have to go out the door, yes let's use that. Come to me. One step in front of the other. Allow the anger to drive you and come to me, Sandy.

18

Tom walks into the living room as Sandy stands. She sees him and Bobby. For a moment she seems very confused. "Tom, what happened?"

"I'm not sure, but let's go back to the dining room, honey."

The anger rises in her again like a flood, "Don't tell me what to do!"

"Okay, sorry hon, I didn't mean to, I just want us to be safe." Tom recognizes the vacancy in her eyes. It's the same emptiness he had seen in Bobby when the vampire had invaded his mind. He immediately knows what he's up against. More than anything, he needs to get her away from the front door. They're too close to the vampire. His mind replays what they had gone through with Bobby in this same position.

"You're a pig, Thomas. A big-headed, giant dumbass pig." Sandy laughs at herself and staggers a little as she takes a step backward toward the front door.

"Yes, I am Sandy, I'm a pig and I'm sorry." He steps forward toward her.

"Piggies are for eating Tommy. That's what we do with big-headed pigs, we eat them." She steps back again. "Do you want us to eat you Tommy do do?"

"Who is 'us' Sandy?"

Sandy stops moving toward the door, confusion painted across her features. "You're trying to trick me and tell me what to do."

"No, I'm asking a question. You said 'us' and I'm asking who you're referring to when you say 'us'". Tom continues to inch forward toward his wife. He wants to keep her talking and distracted.

The look of confusion disappears from Sandy's face, and false confidence replaces it. Tom knows what she's about to do and he's out of time. He throws himself at her when Bobby launches past him toward his mother.

"You aren't going outside mom!" Bobby beats Sandy to the front door and as Sandy is rearing back to hit him, Tom catches her arm and pins it behind her back. Sandy begins screaming in rage and curses him and their son. Little by little, he drags her across the living room to the dining room and as he gains ground the fight drains from her. At the edge of the living room, she goes limp in his arms and the dead weight catches him off guard. He falls into the dining room with Sandy landing on top of him.

"Bobby, help me roll her off of me." The two of them get her flat on her back and he wipes his brow with a sleeve. He's drenched in sweat.

"Thanks for being brave champ, your mom sure needed you back there."

"That's okay dad, I know what it feels like."

Tom pats his son on the back and rubs his shoulder, "What do you mean Bobby?"

"The vampire. He encourages your anger. It feels good. The angrier you get, the more you want to hurt people and it feels good. I know that sounds wrong, and it is, but the truth is acting on your anger feels great. He makes it feel great".

195

19

The husband is becoming quite a problem. Croatoan can feel the familiar rage building.

I had the boy; the door was open and then the man and woman had slammed it shut. And gone was my opportunity to feed. I had the woman; she was right there, and the man ruined that as well.

It's time to abandon the practice of opportunism and become aggressive in his approach to this little clan of humans. If the man is going to ruin every opportunity to feed, perhaps he should remove the man from the situation.

Thomas, I will ensure you suffer as I have this night. When the moment presents itself, I will be there. You are a fine opponent, but you have gained my attention.

With humans, it was always the same. Their weakness is emotion. The sentiment they feel for each other. This man is no exception.

The other two pigs are your weakness, Thomas.

Within the Fog

20

We stay OUT of the living room.

Tom writes this, shows it to both Sandy and Bobby, and taps it with a finger for emphasis. Sandy knows that tap is for her, and she can't disagree. She behaved irrationally and her anger almost got all three of them killed. What she had done was much worse than what Bobby had done. Maybe she should just accept that Tom had his shit together, and she did not. She had to rely on medication to keep her emotional health, and he didn't. It was her that needed his help now, not the other way around. She had fallen right into the vampire's trap. Even after she had seen how he manipulated Bobby, she had gotten angry and done the same thing her eight-year-old son had done. Stupid. She felt a tremendous amount of guilt and was having a hard time looking Tom in the eyes.

She tries whispering to him while staring at her hands. "Tom, I am so sorry. I am. For everything."

"It's okay Sands, it honestly is, we just have to be smart from here on out. And we need to figure out a way to get your medication." Sandy nods her head in agreement. Tom opens his mouth to say something else when he pauses, tilting his head.

"Did you hear that?"

Sandy looks at Bobby, and he looks as puzzled as she feels. "I heard nothing. What was it?"

Just then she hears a knocking sound, very soft, but audible. "Oh no. What is he up to now?"

"It's coming from the back door." Tom jumps up and scurries from the room, and then pokes his head back into the dining room, "Let's stay together as we said, come with me. Both of you."

They all go together and stand in the kitchen listening. Just as Sandy is going to tell Tom she thinks the knocking was coming from somewhere else, they hear it again and she knows he is right; it is definitely coming from the back door. Tom moves to the door, the top of which is covered by a small blue curtain. She fears that if he opens the curtains, they will stare directly into the black eyes of Croatoan.

199

"Tom, just peek out a little. You don't know what he's going to do."

"I don't want to look at all, but I think we need to." Tom takes a deep breath and slowly moves the curtain away from the edge of the window. "Oh wow. I can't believe it."

Tom reaches down and begins disengaging the locks on the back door.

"Tom NO!"

Tom looks over his shoulder, "It's okay Sandy, it's not him. It's a person. It's Sin Roal."

21

"Come in quick Sin." Tom opens the door wide enough for Sin to squeeze through and quietly shuts the door and engages the lock. Sin is wrapped from the top of his head to the floor in blankets. Tom assumes that Sin is using the blankets in the absence of a jacket.

"Sin, how did you get here? Do you know what is out there?"

Sin looks exhausted. Tom wants information from the teenager before he passes out and drops to the floor.

Putting a finger to his lips, Sin says, "Tom, you need to say out loud that you need something from your basement. Say you are going downstairs to get a flashlight or something. You two," Sin motions to Sandy and Bobby, "follow us downstairs."

"Tom, will we be okay downstairs?" Sandy doesn't like this idea at all.

Sin whispers again, "You'll understand soon, but don't worry, they can't come inside unless you let them."

Tom nods to Sandy in agreement. Whatever Sin had to say, he wants to hear it.

22

Sandy is amazed by Sin's ingenuity and intelligence. The three of them stand in the basement. Sin is now only wearing shorts, a t-shirt, and socks. "Sin," she points a finger at the ceiling, "they don't know you're here?"

"That's right, which is why we needed to come down here. I have stopped several times and hid in basements or barns to take off the clothes and blankets so I can cool them down. They cover my body heat, but they also absorb it after a while. It's slow going, but it seems to work. If any of them get too close, though I'll be in trouble. The closer they get, the better they can detect our body heat and get in our minds. I didn't realize it right away, but I figured out it's how they killed my dad. They got inside of his head and made him see things that weren't there. If I can keep going how I was, stopping occasionally to let my blankets and clothes cool down, I can escape the fog and get some help. Oh, and they can fly. It's how they got my dad. Came right down on top of him. I would have been next if I hadn't gone back inside the trailer."

Tom looks to Bobby and back to Sin, "Yeah, we figured out the flying part. The man, the bald man, he had been trying to get Bobby to let him in for several nights. He appeared at Bobby's window on the second floor. We thought Bobby was having nightmares."

Sin looks at Bobby, "I'm sorry you had to go through that. The bald man is the main one of them. He's their leader, but there are more of them. There was a lot of noise coming from town earlier, gunshots and screaming, but it has quieted down. It sounded like there were way more of them in town, but those have gone now. I thought they were all gone, but then I saw him in your front yard. I also saw one going around the corner of your garage, so there are at least a couple of others here with the bald man."

Sandy speaks up, "Sin, we think they are vampires."

Sin replies, "I hadn't thought of that, but that's as good a description as any. But they don't only drink blood. They eat people. They attack in groups and then eat them until nothing remains. I saw Don Hanson in his yard. He was shouting at the bald man and then, boom! It was like they came out of everywhere at the same time and they ate him."

Tom nods in agreement, "We saw the same thing out front. Sabrina Sellers. The bald man was trying to use her to get me to open the door. There were four of them and the bald man."

Sin wipes the back of one hand across his brow, wiping sweat and dirt away, "Be glad you didn't, they would have killed you too. It's why they're out there. They want to eat."

Bobby speaks up for the first time, "I've been telling them that for a few days now."

The little guy seems very sad, and more than a little angry. "Like you guys, I realized they couldn't track my location inside the trailer as long as I kept a window between me and them. I don't know if they forgot about me, or never knew about me. They should have been able to see me when my dad threw me outside. My dad came out after me to...." Sin trails off and based on reputation, Tom can guess what Mearl went after Sin to do.

Sin restarts, "they took my dad, and they were outside for a little while after. I could hear them, but they never tried to contact me. I was behind a window when they were tricking my dad into going outside. I decided that maybe they never knew I was there because I was behind the window and he was behind the door. I'm sure that's how they saw him and not me, although, when I was outside, I'm not sure how they could have missed seeing me. They were flying above us when the bald man attacked my dad. Once I got back inside, I ran from room to room in the trailer. I stayed behind windows grabbing blankets and the clothes. I realized that if they couldn't see me behind the glass I needed to hide my body heat. Listen, I could be wrong about this, but I'm sure we're the only people left alive. At least in the Wray area."

"Oh my God, I hope that's not true. Can that be?" Sandy hadn't even thought about what was going on around them other than what had happened to the Sellers.

"Mrs. Benton, I haven't seen or heard anyone else since the shooting in town stopped. I kept wondering why I hadn't seen a car trying to drive out, or anyone else on foot like me. I think it's because there is no one left alive. They killed everyone but us."

"Sandy, this is how I can get out to the car." Tom points to the blankets laying on the concrete basement floor. "I can put on layers like Sin did and get to the garage and back here fast."

"Oh Tom, I don't know. It seems so risky."
Sandy doesn't want to discuss her medication issues
in front of Sin.

Sin looks from Sandy to Tom, "I wouldn't
do that if I were you. It's slow going because the
clothes and blankets warm up fast. You'd have to be
quick. I mean really quick. The more layers you
wear, the slower you'll move so you need a few
layers to cover your body heat, but not so many
they slow you down. I agree with Mrs. Benton. It's
dangerous."

"Sandy, you know I need to go out there."

Sin recognizes there are things the couple is
leaving out of this discussion because he is present,
so he is quiet. It's their decision, he reasons.

Tom says to Sin, "We have water for you, I
can see you are thirsty. We also have a place to rest
for however long you want. Could I get you to help
me get to the garage, though? I have a good idea,
but I'll need your help."

23

The others in his clan had grown impatient. The woman's body had not provided enough sustenance for the four of them. He had assured them it is only a matter of time before he breaks the minds of the three humans. Despite his reassurances, one male had growled in an attempted show of dominance. Showing not only frustration with a lack of food, but also his strength. While it was not an outright challenge to taking over the leadership of the hunt, it was an affront. This lack of faith he would not accept. Without looking toward the recently turned male, he reached through the veil of the fog and penetrated its mind. He had reached inside of its brain, feeling the hunger and rage, and lashed out with unmatched power. He grasped the essence of the vampire and squeezed until the black inside of it began pouring from its eyes. He could feel it shaking and convulsing as he raised it into the air and then slammed it to the earth, dead. The other three of his clan had slid back into the shadows, fearing his retribution.

There was now one less to feed this night.

24

"If Sin goes upstairs with you two," Tom motions to Sandy and Bobby, "he can be a replacement for me. They don't know that he is here. While you guys are up there carrying on a normal family conversation, I'll wrap up in blankets and get to the garage. It should only take a few minutes."

"But Tom, the vampire will know it's not you if he hears Sin talking." Sandy feels that she is the constant voice of opposition, but Tom's plan scares her.

"Sin won't talk, and you all will stay at the table in the dining room. The bald man, or vampire, won't be close enough to get into any of your minds and Sin just needs to be a body at the table. You and Bobby can talk about something, we'll figure out what that will be, and I'll sneak out the back door. It's our best chance."

Sin looks at the family in front of him and says, "I'll do that as long as it involves a glass of water. I'm parched."

"Of course, Sin, I'm sorry we've been down here so long." Tom realizes he had forgotten Sin needed water.

"I'm so nervous that you're going out there, but it sounds like it should work. But you have to be quick because it won't be realistic for you to be in here sitting at the table saying nothing for long." Sandy feels the weight of responsibility for Tom needing to go outside.

"That's okay mom, I'll go with dad. I'll wrap up so the vampire won't see me either."

"Bobby, I appreciate you wanting to help, but we need all three of you to be here, so the vampire doesn't get suspicious. You have to be inside." Tom pats Bobby on his cheek. He has always loved the soft feel of the boy's skin.

Bobby isn't satisfied with Tom's explanation, "I can say I'm going to go lay down. We already know he couldn't see me through my window. Then I can help you, dad. I'm big enough to go help." Bobby is insulted that Tom won't let him help.

"Listen to me. I'm not telling you this because I don't want your help. I'm saying you need to stay here because having that conversation with your mom is vital to this plan. Sin can't talk, remember. And your mom can't sit and talk to herself."

"Come on dad, you're making excuses. You know I can help you. I want to go with you." Bobby stares at Tom with stubborn insistence.

Sandy grabs Bobby by the shoulders and turns him to face her, "Bobby listen to me. I know you think we don't want your help, but I need you in here with me and it will be faster for your dad if he goes alone. Not to mention I want to know that you're safe." As Bobby begins another round of objections Sandy cuts him off, "And that is final young man. Now let's go upstairs."

In a fit of temper Bobby stamps a foot down to vent his frustration, but it is too late to argue further. Sandy is glaring at him.

Tom looks nervously between his wife and son, "Please Bobby, now is not the time for arguing. We need your help." Satisfied that the issue is resolved, Tom says, "Alright, you all go upstairs. At the table, you and Bobby need to talk about what you would normally talk about."

Sandy gives Tom a long look and thinks again about how much she loves him, because of how much he loves her and their son. "I love you."

"Love you too. I love you too, Bobby."

"Yeah, love you dad."

Sandy and Bobby start up the stairs and Sin glances at Tom as he follows them, "Be careful. Don't move too fast. You don't want to exert yourself and raise your body temperature. I never ran or hurried. I'm not sure how well they hear either, so you need to be quiet. Good luck, Tom. I wish you weren't going out there." With that, Sin is gone. Tom uses the penlight to put on the clothes and blankets Sin has thrown on the floor.

END GAME

1

Tom stands at the back door. Behind him, in the dining room, he can hear Sandy and Bobby talking. She is telling their son how proud she is of him for being such a big kid, and she is asking him what he wants to do for his upcoming birthday party. Tom is pleased with Bobby because he has stopped arguing. Instead, he is helping his mother with their plan. He is chatting right along with her and their conversation sounds normal, believable.

Okay, time to go, he thinks. He pulls one blanket over his head, enough that very little of his face is exposed. He slides the lock on the door and opens it an inch. Peering outside across the patio as far as he can see, which isn't far. The fog is as thick as he's seen it, and that's a good thing. The fog will help him stay unseen. He hates the smell of decay that is a part of the fog, but he will be quick. He plans to go to his right, away from the back of the house and around the hedge. Then straight to the garage by the bank of trees that borders the property. From there, he can use the garage key he has placed in his front right pocket to enter the side door on the garage and get Sandy's medication.

Tom takes a deep breath, wrinkling his nose at the smell, and steps out of the house. He pulls the door shut behind him, hearing it click into place.

2

In the dining room, Sandy chats away with Bobby and Sin sits listening to them. He doesn't want to be rude, but they have forgotten the water, and he feels like he has sand in his throat. Noticing the notepads on the table, he grabs one and scrawls a message to Sandy:

I'm sorry to be a pain, but I really need that water. I'm so thirsty.

Sandy reads his message as she is telling Bobby that he can have a Power Ranger themed birthday party if he wants. She looks at Sin and smacks herself in the forehead for being so forgetful. She mouths the word 'sorry' to Sin. Bobby stops talking and announces to his mom, "I need a glass of water mom, he points to Sin's message, "I'll be right back."

Before Sandy can say she will get it for him, he is off his chair and heading to the kitchen.

"Okay Bobby, be quick."

3

Tom walks at a decent pace, feeling like he needs to run, but resisting the urge, hearing Sin's warning in his head. Go slow. He has cleared the concrete patio and has turned to the left to go around the hedge when he feels a tug at the blanket on his back. His heart rate accelerates until he realizes one of the blankets has gotten caught on a branch protruding from the hedge. He backs up until he can reach the branch. As he is pulling the blanket loose from the branch he freezes, arm in the air, hand in mid grasp. He hears movement and sees the fog swirl about 10 yards ahead. Frozen in place, Tom waits. He is afraid to move as he recalls Sin saying he saw one of the vampires lurking in the backyard. He holds his position for as long as he can until his arm cramps. He removes his blanket from the branch. Listening for a couple of minutes he decides it's as safe as it will get. When all seems still, he resumes his slow walk toward the garage, watching where he places his steps. The last thing he wants to do is trip over something unseen or to snap a twig by stepping on it.

4

The three humans are sitting in the center of the dwelling. He sees their heat at a distance, but they're not nearly as defined as when they come close to him. He hears fragments of their voices, the mother and the son, she is comforting him until he leaves to another room. For a moment he considers moving to the back of the house where the boy has gone, but that may not be necessary. The mother and father sit in silence. This is a good sign. It is a sign that they are weakening and losing their fight. Fear will set in and before too long fear will drive them to surrender. Death becomes a release from the stress and constant worry. Croatoan waits and watches. Soon, he thinks. Soon.

5

Bobby is the slowest kid on earth. Or, he may have wanted to get some time away from his mom. Sin could tell that Bobby was still pissed that he could not go with his dad to the garage. His feet shuffle under the table as he waits in uncomfortable silence for Bobby to return with his glass of water. If it takes much longer, he will go get it from the Benton's kitchen himself. His throat is so dry he can't even swallow his spit. He can hear the voice of his father in his mind, 'Where did that dumb little pecker head go?' He knows it will take a while for Mearl's voice to recede from his thoughts. Mearl was a lot of things, but easy to forget isn't one of them.

Sin shifts his position on the dining room chair. He grows uncomfortable sitting and waiting. Come on kid, by the time you get here I'll need more than a glass of water, I'll need a gallon.

6

Bobby likes Sin, and he feels bad that he is going to leave him thirsty. He doesn't intend to bring Sin any water because he is going to leave. He's tired of his parents considering none of his ideas. He had been waiting for a chance to get to the kitchen and when Sin had written that he was still thirsty on the notepad; he knew it was his chance. He can help his dad and now is his chance to prove it. His mom and Sin would be fine sitting in the dining room. They didn't need him. Quietly, he opens the pantry door in the kitchen, knowing that if he doesn't hurry, he will get caught by his mom. It only takes so long to get a glass of water and return with it, so speed is important. But still he must be quiet enough to not draw his mom's attention. In the pantry's bottom is a box with dust on it. Inside he finds what he is looking for, the picnic table clothes. In Bobby's estimation, these will work fine as a substitute for blankets to cover himself. He wraps several of them around his body, pinching them in the front of himself with his right hand. He doesn't bother shutting the pantry door, fearing the noise it could make. Soon enough both of his parents will figure out he went against their wishes, but by then it will be too late. Whether they thank him for his help or not, they will respect that he is not a baby anymore and that he can be helpful. He could have done the same exact thing Sin had done in sneaking through the mist, and he will prove it.

Bobby has placed the last of the table clothes around his shoulders. He moves to the back door.

7

He is about to clear the last of the hedge and move to the tree line that will lead to the garage when Tom pauses. He will be in the open for at least ten steps when he heads for the trees. Listening carefully, he hears nothing. There is no movement. The fog seems settled and stagnant, and that's as good a sign as he will get to move forward. Stepping out from the protection of the hedge, he reminds himself that slow and steady will win this race. Counting his steps is a way of keeping his imagination in check. One, two…three. As he sets his right foot down for his fourth step, the fog thins. Ahead of him, squatting by the garage, he can see the shape of a man. He knows that what he sees is not a man, but instead one of the vampires. Clad in black, he can see the white skin on the side of its neck and face. This one has a head full of black hair. Tom locks himself in place, knowing that he cannot move at all. He prays that Sin is right about the blankets being enough to shield his body heat from the vampire's senses, or he will soon be dead. Without taking the risk of moving even the position of his head, he focuses his eyes on the shape of the vampire. It sits on its haunches like a dog, sniffing at the mist in front of it. It faces away from him to his left. It sniffs, looks about, and sniffs again. It crawls forward, sniffs again, and lightning-quick turns in his direction, leaping through the air. The vampire lands three feet in front of him. It takes every ounce of Tom's inner strength to keep standing still. If the vampire is smelling him, he is dead. If he moves at all, he will be dead. He holds his breath.

The vampire lifts its head, and it is close enough that Tom can smell the reek of death and see how black its eyes are. They are the black of a starless night in the middle of winter. There is no life within them, and no light from them. They are a void, an empty bottomless pit of despair. He is fascinated by them and feels a little like he is losing his focus. It sniffs again, tilts his head away from Tom, then looks in Tom's direction, sniffs the air one more time and jumps, landing on top of a white and tan rabbit. The rabbit squeals once, and then it is dead, half of its body in one of the vampire's claws, the other half caught in its teeth. Slurping, wet sounds coming from the direction of the vampire and Tom decides this is his best chance to not become a part of its feast.

Moving again, he leaves the sounds of crunching bones behind him. He continues counting his steps in his head, finally allowing himself to breathe. Five, six, seven….

Within the Fog

8

He can't wait any longer for Bobby. Sin grabs the notepad and pen and then holds it under a flashlight for Sandy to read.

Don't you think this is taking too long?

He could tell Sandy had been lost in thought and had no idea how long Bobby had been gone. After reading his note, she looks panicked. She rises and heads to the kitchen, and Sin follows her in the hopes of finally getting some water.

9

Bobby peers through the crack he has created by opening the back door. He can't see anything beyond the wall of fog. He figures if he saw a vampire outside, he would shut the door fast, but it looks clear. He should be able to catch up with his dad. He moves to the left of the door frame. He needs room to pull the door open so he can get outside. If he didn't have to worry about the vampire hearing him, he would go outside and then call for his dad to wait for him. That's okay, he reasons, I can move faster than my dad since I'm smaller than him. With that, Bobby opens the back door and steps into the fog.

10

Croatoan watches the red blurs of the
mother and father stand and move quickly. They go
to the small red blur, the boy, in the other room.
He perks up when he realizes the boy is opening a
door to the outside, on the other side of the house.
The boy is trying to get outside. They are breaking.
The large wings on his back open and then push
toward the earth. Like a great eagle, he launches
into the air over the house.

11

Arriving at the side door to the garage, Tom uses the key and enters the garage and then re-closes the door. As fast as he can he takes the blankets off, and a layer of clothes. He has a little time to cool them down while he gets Sandy's prescription from the outback. The Outback door hatch opens, and he cringes as the exterior lights flash. He decides he will leave the hatch hanging open so that the lights won't flash again. Staring into the back of the car, he can tell his wife was in a hurry to load everything she bought at Sanders market. Items are thrown throughout the storage area in the back of the vehicle. A quick sorting through canned goods, propane, and bottled water leads him to the pharmacy bag. He opens it up, withdraws the small bottle of pills, and tucks it into the pocket on the front of his shirt.

With remorse, he turns away from the contents of the vehicle. He wishes he could bring the bottled water back with him. They have only one case of bottled water in the house and he can't believe he let their supply run that low. As long as he had been preparing for an emergency, he knew better than to run low on bottled water.

Back by the side door in the garage, he puts the clothes back on and layers the blankets over his back and head. The clothes feel damp with sweat, but they also feel cool. The blankets will heat faster as he returns from the garage since he doesn't have the time to completely cool them down. With a little luck, he won't run into the dark-haired vampire on his way back. He is sure that pissing down his leg will not help him hide from the heat-seeking monster.

12

One step out the door. He hears nothing at all. The world is quieter than he has ever heard. The quiet is good, and bad. Good, because he can't hear any monsters, bad because there is no noise to cover his steps. For the first time, it occurs to him he shouldn't be out here trying to find his dad. Then he thinks if he chickens out, he will only prove that he is the big baby his parents think he is. Then they'll never listen to him. With a renewed commitment to finding his dad, he takes his next step when both of his feet leave the ground and he feels himself being jerked back inside the kitchen.

"What the hell do you think you're doing?" His mother towers over him. She is red with anger and she is doing her best to keep her voice to a whisper.

"I'm sorry mom, I wanted to go with dad."

"You're sorry? How many times do you need to be told that you need to listen to what your father and I tell you? Will you also be sorry if your dad dies out there because you can't follow simple instructions?"

Bobby's eyes well up with tears. "If he dies, it's your fault. It's your stupid medicine he's out there trying to find. I just wanted to help."

Sin is pushing the back door shut as Bobby lashes out a leg to get to his feet. As he does, his shoe hits the edge of the door and it prevents the door from completely closing.

"Don't you speak to me that way. If we weren't trying to survive the end of the world, I would give you the spanking of your life. You will get to the damn dining room table and you will carry the conversation your dad asked us to have until he gets back here."

Sandy grabs her son by his neck after peeling the table clothes off him. She marches him back to the dining room.

Jesus, Sin thinks I'm not going to die at the hands of the vampires, I'm going to die of thirst.

13

The fog scatters around him as he lands in the backyard next to the long row of a hedge. The boy and the parents had been at the back door, but now they are gone. He sees them as red blurs, so they have once again moved back to the center of the dwelling. Fearing a trap of some sort, he pushes closer to the house along the row of vegetation. Something is wrong with the back door. From his angle, he peers across the porch and can see into the home. The door is slightly open, and the humans are not near it.

14

Tom thinks it has taken him far too much time to get back to the patio, but he has finally arrived. He didn't see the dark-haired vampire again, but he knows that there are more than one or two of the creatures lurking in the fog. Several light steps bring him across the concrete surface. He approaches the back door and reaches for the handle when he realizes he can see into the dark cavern of the kitchen. The door is open a crack. Tom pauses, feeling indecision. He needs to get in out of the fog. But why is the door open?

15

"Well, I think we will all look forward to your birthday party Bobby, it sounds like it will be fun."

Bobby stares across the table at his mother, no longer willing to play the game.

Whispering, she leans close to her sons' ear, "Straighten out your attitude. When your dad..."

Sandy cuts herself off as the three of them hear a slight creaking sound. The back door. They sit at the table, listening intently. Sin knows he and Tom will need to go back to the basement so he can put the blankets back on. Of course, they will need to cool down again for a while first. The sooner he can get back outside, the sooner he will get out of the fog and find help.

They sit and listen and hear nothing further.

16

Tom stares at the open back door and feels a massive weight on his shoulders. His heart pounds in his chest. Several thoughts converge in his mind at the same time; Dammit, I thought I got this closed. How could I have not gotten the door shut?

He stands staring as the door slowly swings into the darkness of the kitchen. He steps inside when the memory of stepping out of the kitchen slams back into his mind. I shut the door. I heard it click shut. I remember.

He peers into the interior of the house and listens. Nothing. No sound emerges. He steps fully inside and pushes the door closed behind him. His legs carry him to the edge of the dining room. Still no sound.

Reaching into his pocket, he grabs the penlight and shines it into the room. The dining chairs greet him, but they do not explain their empty seats.

He risks calling out to his family and Sin, although as quietly as he can, "Hello?"

No response. His gut is telling him there is great danger here, but his rational mind dismisses this internal claim. He had a plan. Get the medicine so that Sandy will feel better and get back safely. He has done that. Now they can wait out this situation safely in the comfort of their home. Eventually, someone will come to help them, or the vampires will leave. Dawn can only be a few hours away. They have to be okay after all they've gone through today. They have to be.

"Sandy? Bobby? Where are you?"

Nothing.

"Shit, shit, shit."

Moving further into the dining room, he finally hears something, although it is not a voice. He stops moving and listens intently. The sound has stopped. This is not right.

Standing in the dark, the house is as silent as a tomb. His breath is all he can hear, so he holds it. There, the sound comes through the dark again. It is a thump followed by a soft dragging sound. There is a pause and then he hears it again. Thump, drag. Pause. Thump, drag. The dragging sound is lasting longer, and it is getting louder, closer. He shines his penlight straight ahead, only slightly piercing the

235

darkness, and moves from the dining room into the living room. The noises are coming from the opposite side of the living room. He moves in that direction and stops to listen again. Thump, drag.

The hallway.

He turns his small light on the hallway in time to see Sandy step into the living room on her left leg, drag her right leg behind her, and collapse to the floor. He runs a few quick steps to her and kneels by her side. She is bleeding from her side, where the fabric of her tan colored blouse is shredded. She is laying on her back and the right side of her face is so swollen that he only knows it is her by the color of her eyes. Her leg is shattered and deformed. Blood pools in her shoe and her right leg is twice the size of the other one.

"Tom, he…" She takes a deep breath, and it does not sound good. Not at all. It sounds as though she is trying to breathe air through a filter filled with mud.

"Oh, my God. Sandy, It's going to be okay, I'll get you to the car. We can get into town to the emergency room. Hang on honey, I'll get Bobby and…." Tom looks down the hallway, it is empty. "Where's Bobby?"

Sandy pulls in a deep, wet breath, "Tom, you don't... understand.... it's..." Her breath leaves her, and she coughs a little and tries to pull in more air.

"Shhhh, I'll get him, and we'll get out of here. Bobby!" Tom calls out to their son. Tears are rolling down his face because deep inside he knows she doesn't have long. He doesn't know much about emergency medicine, but Sandy's breathing is tearing at his soul. He loves her so much. He will save her.

"Bobby dammit, come out here, we have to leave, NOW!"

"Tom, it's not .... he's..... it's him...."

The vampire. Tom knew from the moment he saw her fall to the floor. The vampire.

The air at Tom's back feels chilled. It grows colder by the second. He smells the earthy scent of the fog. His head begins itching, and he involuntarily digs at his right temple. Tom staggers to his feet and looks into the large mirror that has been on this living room wall since they had moved into the house. It had already been here when they moved in, and Sandy loved it. They kept it on this wall as she wished. He sees himself, blankets falling off his shoulders and no one else. He looks past his reflection in the depths of the mirror. No one.

Inside his head, a voice emerges.

You should have listened to me. It's your fault.

"Oh no, no. Please, no."

Tom slowly turns his body to face the room behind him.

Looking down, he sees the white skin. Blue veins pulsing just beneath his familiar soft cheeks. The sheen on those cheeks. Tom looks into his eyes. They have gone black.

Hi daddy.

The End – Book 1

Book 2 – Rage Within the Fog – now available on Amazon

Thank you

Thank you for reading Within the Fog, book one. It is my intent to entertain my readers and hopefully I have accomplished that in this book. While Wray, CO is a real town, all the locations and business names, as well as the characters are fictitious and in no way related to the real town of Wray (Unless Croatoan is lurking somewhere in the shadows on the plains of Colorado). The settlement of the Roanoke Island Colony in 1587 was a reality, and so was the disappearance of 115 people from that colony shortly after John White returned to England for supplies. Where did those settlers go? No one knows for certain. The word Croatoan was indeed carved into wood at the Roanoke settlement. Was Croatoan really a vampire who destroyed the colony and, with his clan, consumed every soul?

I'll leave that to you to determine.

Within the Fog was born from a curiosity I have long held.

What is it that lurks within the fog?

The nights the fog rolls in thick and heavy, the air is still, and you peer out your windows. Is the figure you see hiding in the shadows your imagination?

Is something out there looking back at you?

My guess is the answer is, yes, and it has fangs.

I have only two requests of you my fellow reader of horror. Please return for part two, and **PLEASE** take a moment to write a review on Amazon. The reviews are the most important tool I have to know my audience. Also, I would love to invite you to join our **Preferred Reader Club and Newsletter** at www.withinthefogbook.com

Since the completion of *Within the Fog*, I have completed the second book in the trilogy, *Rage Within the Fog*. Please enjoy the first couple of chapters of *Rage* next!

Thank you again for reading.

See you soon.

Charles Welch

8/29/2020

RAGE

Within the Fog

Lake Angikuni, Nunavut, Canada 1930 – SEPTEMBER

1

Amaruq kneels beside his wife's fresh grave with his two daughters, eight-year-old Akna, who looks exactly like her mother with her raven black hair, and four-year-old Kireama, who looks nothing like her mother. Kireama doesn't look exactly like her father either, and he recalls how he had teased his wife about that, often asking her who she had invited into their Tupiq when he wasn't looking. She would laugh at him and tell him it was a fleeting romance with Joe, their fur trapper friend. Joe was a much older, western pale man and Kireama was a very dark-skinned girl. He cherishes the memories he has of laughing with her about that. Amaruq looks at both of his daughters, who wipe tears from their eyes. They recite the blessing of the dead prayer for their mother. A week ago, she had been standing with them in the burial ground, praying for their ancestors to watch over them. Now they prayed to ask the same of her.

A few days after praying in the burial grounds with his wife, her ancestors had called her to join them in the afterlife. She died fevered and delusional, crying out in the night. Her cries were filled with warnings that they beware of the coming wrath. She whispered to Amaruq, telling him to protect their daughters from the pale man who would drain them of their blood and consume them whole.

Amaruq is not a man given to superstition, but his wife's cries had a chilling effect on him. After her passing, he read the stars for signs of coming trouble and inspected the frozen ground in the mornings for the footprints of a nightwalker, or worse yet, Adlet. Although he kept this to himself, word of his wife's fever dreams had spread through the tribe and he was not oblivious to the other men who casually inspected the same ground as he each morning.

Their prayers complete, Amaruq stands and instructs his daughters to step back. The members of the community begin the tradition of placing stones on the gravesite. This is done to prevent the dead from rising and becoming a nightwalker. It is a large pile of stones and takes some work for the community to get them all in place. For the previous two days, the thirty members of the tribe had been digging the stones from the earth in preparation of the ceremony. In keeping with tradition, the last stones to be placed upon the pile are those offered by the grieving family. It is their way of saying goodbye. These stones have been selected by each family member because they felt a connection between the stone and the deceased. The stones are from the earth, and their mother's body will return to the earth.

Amaruq's daughters place their stones side by side and proclaim their never-ending love for their mother. He places his stone and simply says, "Nuliiq", the Inuit word for wife. He turns to face the tribe and offers his thanks to them. In a month, the elderly women of the tribe will begin hinting at him to take an interest in their daughters, but he has no taste for an arranged marriage. Asiaq was the love of his life, and one does not recover from such a loss so quickly.

The tribe Angakkuq, their spiritual leader, begins leading the tribe to the life celebration feast. Amaruq will not eat, as is customary of the spouse in such circumstances, but he has instructed his daughters to partake in honor of their mother. As he makes his way to his seat of honor amongst the tribe, he cannot help but wonder if Anguta the God of the dead, has already gathered his wife to be with the rest of their ancestors.

"Ataata, can I finish the repair of my clothing after the feast?" Akna looks to Amaruq with large brown eyes that are tinged with the red of sadness.

"Yes, little flower, there will be time for our work, but tonight is for honoring your mother. Her beautiful soul now flies with our ancestors. It is our responsibility to make sure we express our love of her to the tribe so that she may leave knowing our peace."

Akna nods her head, but still seems lost. She has yet to accept her mother's loss.

"Ataata, when will Anaana move on? Will the fog leave the woods with her?"

Amaruq stops walking and turns Akna by her shoulders to face him. "What fog in the woods? Where did you see fog?"

"Kireama and I walked through the woods to the river overlook before the burial ceremony. There is fog gathering on the other side of the river."

2

Amaruq sits before a roaring fire, next to the Angakkuq listening to his blessing of their meal. When the old man has finished, Amaruq whispers into his ear. He tells him of the fog that his daughters have seen by the river. The old man's eyebrows slowly rise. Fog is an omen of darkness and death. Whenever fog gathers, the Inuit shelter within their Tupiq waiting for it to pass. They hide from fog, praying it will move on with no loss of life within the tribe, but it is Adlet who they truly fear. The God-like cannibal travels in a shroud of fog.

The Angakkuq stands and all eyes are on him. "We will all celebrate Asiaq on our own tonight. Please gather your food and return to your Tupiq. There is fog gathering by the river." Quiet murmurings spread through the tribe like a ripple across a pond. No doubt they are whispering not only of the fog, but also of the fevered warnings of Asiaq.

"Quickly."

The people of the tribe rise and begin gathering food and drink. People are trying not to show the panic they feel, but Amaruq can smell their fear. He turns to his daughters, "Take enough food for tonight and tomorrow and go to the Tupiq. I'll be with you shortly."

"But Ataata, where will you go?"

"I will tie the dogs up by the lake and return to you. Do not be worried, we have no fog in the village yet, and even if it comes, it will likely pass with no trouble."

Akna is not satisfied. "What about the dogs, won't they be safer in the Tupiq with us? Nightwalkers will eat the dogs."

"No honey, nightwalkers are only interested in animals when they are near humans. If they are separate, they will be safer." He smiles at his daughters, "But let me ask you a question. Have you ever seen a nightwalker?"

Both daughters speak in unison, "No Ataata. But the Angakkuq said…"

"He said for us to be safe due to the coming fog. We are just being cautious."

"Yes, but Ataata, nightwalkers are not all we fear."

"Yes, I know. Want to know a secret?"

Both daughters nod enthusiastically, particularly little Kireama.

"Well, as it turns out, I have never seen a nightwalker, or Adlet. Now off with you both. Get the food and go straight to the Tupiq."

"Aww, Ataata, we want a real secret. That's not a secret!" Kireama stamps her foot to emphasize her frustration.

"I will tell you a real secret tonight after we eat, as long as you are both in the Tupiq before I return from taking the dogs to the lake."

"Promise?" This time it is Akna who gazes at him.

"I promise."

3

The dogs are unsettled and barking at the tree line behind the camp. They stare into the forest as though an invisible enemy waits there for them, calling. The wind has picked up in the short time that Amaruq has taken to gather the dogs on their leashes. Amaqiuaq, one of Amaruq's closest friends, approaches and offers his help with the dogs.

"Are you taking them to the lake?"

"Yes, they will be better off away from camp if..." Amaruq trails off and Amaqiuaq nods his head in agreement.

"Brother, listen, I haven't had a chance to tell you how sorry I am about the loss, our loss, of Asiaq. My prayers are that she is watching over us with the ancestors."

Amaruq winces when he hears his wife's name for what feels like the thousandth time since her passing. "Thank you, brother."

Amaqiuaq nods again. "This fog is a bad omen. The dogs are upset. They sense something. Have your weapon prepared." Both men speak hushed words of reassurance to the dogs in an attempt at calming them. They pay them no attention, however, continuing to focus their growls of uneasiness at the surrounding trees.

"I have thought of that already and I agree, there is something in the air. Terrible energy surrounds us. The building presence of fog is the reason. We must be vigilant throughout this night. I hope it is not Adlet, coming to punish us."

"If Adlet comes, our weapons will not matter. The legends say that Adlet is indestructible. We will pray it is not he who comes with the fog." Amaruq remembers the legends of the blood-drinking, Inuit consuming cannibal. As a child, he heard from tribe elders all about Adlet. Although, in those days, his grandmother told him the story as a method of motivating him to go to bed. She would pinch his ear and steer him to his blankets saying, "Little Amaruq, be wise and go to bed before Adlet arrives in his cloud of fog to eat you up!"

"We will pray tonight for Torngarsuk to protect us. The sky God is the only way to defeat Adlet."

As they finish tying the dogs to the tree stump by the lake, Amaqiuaq pulls a short-pointed shaft of carved tree limb from the waste of his pants. "Here, brother. Keep this. We will pray to Torngarsuk, but perhaps he is not the only way to defeat Adlet, if indeed Adlet arrives this night."

"This is only legend, Amaqiuaq." Amaruq shakes the small spear at him. "We do not know if Adlet is coming with the fog, and even if he is, we do not know if piercing him with wooden spears offers any help in defeating his threat." Amaruq hands the spear back to his friend, who in return pushes the spear back at Amaruq.

"Legend or not, keep it. Just in case. I have one as well. Better to have some hope, than none."

Amaruq smiles and thanks his friend for his thoughtfulness. He walks back to his Tupiq thinking that if he really finds a need for the spear on this night; they are indeed in a lot of trouble.

4

After arriving at his Tupiq, Amaruq hangs his caribou skin coat on one of the tall support poles and sits next to his worrying daughters. He is glad that he had tucked the weapon given to him by Amaqiuaq inside of the coat. The last thing his girls need to see is an additional weapon in their home. They have prepared him a bowl of stew and he eats more as a courtesy to them than he does out of hunger.

"Ataata, are you also worried tonight?" Akna asks him this as she shovels in her last bite of dinner.

"No, my little worrywart. I am not. Hopefully, we will not even see the fog make its way to our village tonight. But if it does, let us not forget, this is not the first fog to appear here, and it won't be the last."

"Ataata, it is not the fog that worries me but the Adlet that travels within." Kireama's eyes are as big as the bowl she nibbles from.

"Who is it that speaks of Adlet on such a night as this?"

"Everyone. Ataata, everyone in the village fears Adlet on this night, and…" She looks to her sister, "We are worried as well."

"My daughter's, we have had such a hard week. This fog is just that, fog. We should offer a prayer of protection to Torngarsuk and then you two should get ready to sleep. We will quit worrying and do our best to love each other as your mother would want."

Akna interrupts her father, "Ataata, you said I could finish my clothing repairs before bed."

"Yes, of course, and then off to bed." It occurs to him that his daughters will now need to grow up quickly. The clothing repair was something Asiaq would take care of if she were still alive. It is good that she had taught her daughters such things as stitching before her passing.

While his daughters are busy repairing the clothing, he checks his rifle. It is loaded and leaning by the entry flap to the Tupiq. He sits near the weapon watching his girls work while they whisper their conspiratorial secrets to each other. Occasional giggles emanate across the space between them and he thinks that if his wife is watching over them, she is very happy. How happy she would be to see their daughters so close. They are fortunate to have each other, he thinks.

His eyes blink shut, and he feels the warm drift of a sleepy tide pulling at him. He knows he should open his eyes, but he wants to ride in this comfort for a few moments. It has been a rough few days, and moments of peace such as this have been fleeting. In his mind, he can hear his wife calling to him. He listens, knowing it is her voice, wondering what she will tell him. Come closer, he thinks to her. Come sit by me, my love, and tell me the secrets of the afterlife. He hears her calling his name. It is too far away at first.

"Amaruq." She is so far away and her voice trails, drifting.

"Amaruq." Even softer, her voice is so faint, and he again calls out to her to come closer.

"ATAATA!" He jumps awake, back to reality, and stares into the faces of his little girls. Both of their mouths hang open and they are pointing to the entry to the Tupiq. He turns toward their pointing to stare at the closed caribou flap that separates them from the elements outside. He sees small wispy tendrils of vapor leaking inside the gap between the caribou flap and the wall of the Tupiq.

"Ataata, it is fog. It has arrived."

From somewhere in the village, Amaruq and his daughters hear a scream, the first of many.

Wray, Colorado, 2019 — July

1

Tom sits next to his wife's body in the hallway of his home. He holds her hand and tells her he will figure everything out, that it will all be okay. He insists he will find a way to save their son Bobby. His dried tears leave crusty tracks down his cheeks. He does not mind or notice them. The fog shroud that smells of death and rot continues to smother and suffocate outside of his home. The fog is a haven for Croatoan and is where his son is now. Bobby is with Croatoan in the fog because Croatoan bit and infected Bobby. He is unsure if that happened before or after Croatoan mortally wounded his wife.

"I'll get Bobby back and get the infection out of him. There has to be a way and I'll find it." He pats her hand, which has grown cold and stiff, although he does not notice that either. "I still need you, Sandy, so much. I don't know how to live without you, but I promise you, I'll make sure Bobby grows up as we planned."

Renewed tears free themselves and follow their predecessors down his face, winding their way through the forest of beard stubble and fall onto his shirt, staining it with grief.

"I'm so sorry, honey. I didn't want this, and now I don't know what I'll do without you. And Bobby... I'll get him back babe, I swear I will." Sandy does not respond to him and hasn't since she tried to warn him about Bobby.

Despite the evil operating within the fog, he had gone to the garage for her medicine. She had left it in her Subaru. She needed it because without it she couldn't think straight. Without Xanax she could become very depressed, even after only a short time. Even though his house is surrounded by a fog bank that is a host to the worst kind of evil, he had known he had to take the risk to retrieve her medication.

"We both thought I should get the medication," Tom says this in defense of himself, even though there is no one offering criticism.

Somehow, Croatoan, the bald, pale demon, had gained entry to their home in his absence. He had killed his wife and bitten his only child, Bobby, who now wandered within the fog like the lost soul he had become.

Sin, the teenage son of the town drunk, had shown up in the middle of their standoff with Croatoan. He had cloaked himself in blankets so that the vampires could not see him. Sin had figured out that the vampires couldn't see you if they couldn't see your body heat. When Sin had shown up, Tom had his answer. He knew how to get to the garage to retrieve Sandy's medication. He had left Sandy and Bobby with Sin posing in his place to retrieve her medication.

Tom reaches a hand up and feels the pill bottle in his shirt pocket. He had forgotten all about the medication once he had returned to the house from the garage. On his approach to the house, he realized the back door was slightly open. Croatoan and the other vampires couldn't gain entry without being let inside. They couldn't drain the blood from a human and completely consume a human's body without getting in or getting the human to come outside.

While Tom and his family had been hiding inside, Croatoan had reached inside of Bobby and Sandy's minds. He had manipulated them to get them to come outside, and it had almost worked. Both Sandy and Bobby had almost opened the door to their home, with Croatoan waiting on the other side. They had twice narrowly averted disaster, only to see Croatoan gain entry in Tom's absence. When Tom had returned from the garage and had seen the back door open a crack, he had at first questioned whether it had been he who had failed to close the door. Once inside, he knew he had not left the door open. Something had happened while he was in the garage that created the opening Croatoan needed.

Back inside the house, he had come face to face with his eight-year-old son. He had seen Bobby's snow white skin and knew in his gut what had happened before Bobby had reached inside of his mind to speak to him. When Bobby forced his way into Tom's mind, he found out more than he had ever wanted to know. By the time he had fought Bobby off and thrown him out the front door, Sandy had died. He shudders, thinking about the cold feel of Bobby's skin as they had wrestled, rolling toward the front door. God, Bobby had become incredibly strong.

He looks at Sandy's swollen face and remembers how afraid she had been to have him leave for her medication. She had asked him to hurry back and told him she loved him, and he loved her too, now that she was gone, more than ever.

"I love you, honey, and I always will." Tom leans down and kisses his wife's forehead. He marvels at how strange he feels. A day before, his life was exactly as he wanted it. He had a nice, remote job with a large company that paid well. His schedule was his own, working when it was most convenient so that he could enjoy his family and take part in his son's life as he grew up. They had moved from Denver to the small Eastern Colorado town of Wray to slow down the pace of life and to have time to enjoy one another. His marriage had improved, he had been working on his relationship with Bobby and everything had been pointing up. Then yesterday evening, a strange fog had gathered over the town and had spread throughout his neighborhood. What had come to them from inside the fog bank had been pure devastation.

Bobby had warned him and Sandy. He had seen the man within the fog outside of his second-story bedroom window for several nights. Bobby had begged them to believe him, implored them to listen to him. Instead of taking Bobby seriously, he and Sandy had dismissed his son's claims as those of a young boy suffering from night terrors. That dismissal had cost his wife her life and had caused his son a different death. The son he had confronted when returning to the house from the garage was no longer the sweet little boy he had raised. He was an angry, venomous monster who had tried to kill him.

Tom rocks back and forth without realizing he is doing so, working out pent up energy and anger. He tries to find a way to save his son, while trying to say everything to Sandy that his heart desires to express. Even though she slipped away while he was defending himself against what was left of Bobby, he wants to tell her how much he has always loved her.

"Sandy, I love you so much. If I lose Bobby too, there will be nothing left for me. I have to save him. Without you and him, I will be lost. For you, and me, I'll do everything I can to save him. I don't know where to begin honey, but I'll figure something out." Tom continues to rock back and forth. He pats his wife's hand, her arm, and back to her hand.

"I promise, I'll get Bobby back. There must be some kind of medical research or something that can help him, if I can catch him and get him to a hospital." He wracks his brain, trying to figure out a way to get to Bobby without Croatoan knowing. The old vampire is powerful, and Tom knows he will not survive a confrontation with Croatoan. "That's what I'll do. Sandy, I'm going to save our son. I'll get him help. I'll find a way."

Behind Tom, in the living room, a floorboard creaks, and he freezes. He knows he never got the back door shut. He waits for that all too familiar cold sensation of something burrowing into his head. It's how the dead that roam the fog communicate straight into the brain. He waits for another sound or the invasion of his mind. Neither comes. Then, with his ears, not his mind, he hears a voice. It is soft sounding.

"If you want Bobby back, I think there is only one way."

Tom turns toward the voice, "Sin?"

Sin is standing in the shadows of the living room, wrapped in blankets. "We have to kill him. We will have to kill Croatoan, and I think we need to do it before Bobby can feed."

Tom carefully places Sandy's hand back on the hallway floor. He closes her eyes with his fingertips. The anger in Tom pushes him to his feet. "Where were you, Sin? Where were you while Sandy was being mauled and Bobby was being bitten?"

ABOUT THE AUTHOR

Charles Welch lives in Greeley, CO. He is a former public-school teacher and holds an M.Ed. in Learning and Technology and an Ed.D. in eLearning. He lives with his wife Mia and has 3 children, 5 god children and 3 grandchildren. His passions include the Denver Broncos, reading the masters of horror and watching every scary movie he can.

Printed in Great Britain
by Amazon

33692251R00145